THE GREAT CANADIAN ADVENTURE:

From Indian Country To Nation State

ISBN: 1500741825
ISBN 13: 9781500741822

THE GREAT CANADIAN ADVENTURE:

From Indian Country To Nation State

Rosemary I Patterson Ph.D.

Many Thanks to MaryEllen Campbell for her suggestions and her loan of relevant books including "Through The Mackenzie Basin: A Narrative of the Athabasca and Peace River Treaty Expedition of 1899" By Charles Mair, English Secretary of the Half-Breed Commission. Toronto, William Briggs, 1908.

TABLE OF CONTENTS

Chapter 1. The Numbered Treaties.

Katherine Golden Eagle shook her head in disbelief as she wearily left her ox- drawn replica of a Red River Cart and sank gratefully to the ground. The screech of the wheels of the cart (wood on wood) was agonizing to her nerves. The Red River Cart ride, documenting some of the routes of the numbered Treaty makers in the late 1800's, through what are now most of Manitoba, Saskatchewan, Alberta, The Northwest Territories and part of British Columbia, was jarring and causing the back injury she had received during a College basketball game to act up. Kate, as the tall, strikingly beautiful graduate student was called, had been recruited by George McBay, the handsome son of a wealthy businessman and CEO of a promising film company.

Kate had been recruited as a result of her photogenic, First Nations looks to be an extra in a documentary concerning the making of the numbered Treaties 5, 6, 7 and 8 in the 1870's to late 1890's that transferred ownership of the huge area known as Rupert's Land to the new government of the Dominion of Canada.

Oh No! Some part of Kate's mind was panicking. My Sciatica Nerve is twinging. It causes excruciating pain. I'll never get up from the ground. They'll have to carry me into someone else's cart and into a plane back to a hospital for the back surgery I refused. Kate forced herself to shift into the position that usually stopped the twinging, her left leg raised somewhat and her body in complete stillness. *It's working,* she sighed to herself. *Thanks Great Spirit or Great Mystery, I really need the money from this job to keep paying my student fees.* Kate had never managed to know who for sure she was contacting on the other side but from her own experience, which she hesitated to tell to anyone as people did not validate subjective experiences anymore, she knew that some kind of higher power came to her aid when she needed it the most.

The Numbered Treaties transferred vast areas of land from the First Nations people who had occupied it for centuries and legally (as far as Euro-centric people were concerned) made it available for the myriads of settlers that would be brought in from all over Europe. The settlers were deemed necessary to keep the land in British hands rather than it becoming American. By 1869 it was known that lucrative resources existed in the huge expanse of land and British capitalists were already eager for access to its riches before what were now Americans succeeded with their plans to take over the vast area.

The only problem was that the Plains Indians were still strong and capable of resistance once they realized the hunting and gathering lands they had used for centuries were being overrun by settlers and their food supplies, the Bison and the Passenger Pigeon, were being deliberately eliminated by bounty hunters in the U.S. The Americans were also mercilessly killing and moving the rightful owners of their lands west with Indian wars being fought by the American Calvary costing twenty million dollars a year. John A. MacDonald would try treaty making instead with the Indians in the new Dominion of Canada still loyal to the British Crown after fighting for them during the French Indian Wars, the American Revolution and the War of 1812.

The Americans had long sought all of Canada to create a vast empire stretching from the Gulf of Mexico to the Arctic Circle. The Americans fervently believed it was their "Manifest Destiny" as descendants of the white, Superior, Christian race. Of course, as Vine Deloria Jr., the influential Indian historian and Kate's favorite author, pointed out, they were descended from the criminals sent over from England for the Penal Colony, indentured servants, and or/ fanatical Christians, what did they know?

In March 1867 the U.S Secretary of State, Seward, had negotiated the purchase of Alaska from Russia, hoping its acquisition would lead to obtaining all the land in North America. He urged an American banker to buy out the rights of the Hudson's Bay Company in Rupert's Land. In December 1867, a US Senate bill was passed authorizing the takeover of all territory west of Thunder Bay, and also authorizing six million dollars to buy out the Hudson's Bay Company, to take over British Columbia debt and to build a railway to Puget Sound thereby guaranteeing that the U.S. would own all of Canada west of Thunder Bay as well as all that it had obtained through diplomatic means.

The Treaty of Ghent to end the War of 1812 had given the U.S. all the Indian Country along the Ohio, Mohawk and Mississippi River Systems. Great Britain negotiators had betrayed the Iroquois Confederation allies of the British who lived in the vast areas and had fought for them. Loyal members of the Iroquois Federation had many times saved the British Regulars, French Canadians and even German mercenaries fighting for the British from certain defeat. Many Iroquois fled to Canada to avoid the Long knives of the U.S. Calvary while the Creeks, Chickasaws, Cherokees, Choctaws, and Seminoles were forced west of the Mississippi to Oklahoma and beyond. In 1859 another treaty gave the U.S. the Oregon Territory on the West Coast even though non-Indian occupation had been in Hudson's Bay Company's hands through its fur trading forts.

Kate let out a deep sigh as she mused over her knowledge of this time era.

I guess it's a good thing that the U.S. did not succeed with its plans to absorb all of Canada into its North American empire. John A. McDonald beat them to it with the British North America Act in 1868 creating the Dominion of Canada and the transfer of the Hudson's Bay Companies' lands to the new Dominion for three million dollars. Otherwise the Plains Indians would likely have been hunted and shot on sight as was done by Americans after Mexico lost California. It's hard to believe that fifty thousand Indians were shot deliberately by bounty hunters for the $100.00 bounty on men and $50.00 bounty on women to clear out that area for American settlers. But what would you expect from a country that had imported ten million slaves to work their vast sugar cane and cotton plantations.

For the documentary that Kate had been hired for as an extra, thirteen Red River Carts, several York boats and numerous scows were being filmed carrying First Nations and other actors through parts of what were back then the wild lands and rivers of what was left of Indian Country soon to become Western and Northern Canada, the key locations of the treaty maker's journeys. Gold had been found in the Yukon, vast oil deposits in the Mackenzie and Athabasca river basins, and the necessity of building a railroad across the Plains made it mandatory to remove the lands (or so believed John A. MacDonald and his cabinet) from their rightful owners, the Cree, Blackfoot, Ojibwa, Inuit, Dene and many other Indian and Inuit Nations.

Already I'm physically and mentally done, Kate mused to herself again, *and depressed. We are only at the start of the journey and my Sciatica nerve is twinging. I never realized how grueling the voyage was going to be and I'm so tired of trying to prove myself to white people. It's been the same all my life. While at least we are not shot on sight any more, many white people look at me, a Mohawk/Cree descendant, and immediately I can see on their faces they are trying to ascertain if I fit in with their stereotypes of Indians. Is she one of those lazy Indians, I can see them think.*

Or does she belong to those alcoholic families that we see living in the slums of Winnipeg? Or is she one of those violent Mohawk people that resisted the rightful authority of the Canadian government in Oka, Quebec, when all they wanted was to dig up the Indian graveyard to build onto a golf course. Or with whites of the opposite sex, is she one of those exotic but promiscuous Indian women we can easily take advantage of and manipulate. Or what are those Indians still doing here? I thought they were all supposed to have died off years ago so we wouldn't have to feel guilty about taking their land.

You immediately try and counteract their negative reaction by using some of the educational jargon you have picked up in your College and University years, some part of Kate's mind seemed to be talking to her, *and that seems to help somewhat. It was worse in Elementary and High School. There you were always being judged as being somehow less than most of the white students. For years you have been over achieving to compensate.*

And your love relationships, if you can all them that. You've managed to have your heart broken already by two youths, one recently, a white, College fellow, and one a First Nations young man. You were dazzled by their looks. You really have to get over equating handsome with predestined soul mate. For the white fellow you were just an example of exotic love to be placed besides the notches on his gun barrel of conquests and your love was not enough to stop the First Nations one from suicide.

Oh My God! Kate sighed to herself. *No wonder I've concentrated on my university studies after my back injury ended my quest to be accepted by white people as an outstanding Basketball player. Now if I can only get back to my studies. If only I hadn't needed the money to help with student loans. The three things constant in my life in Canada are grinding poverty, identity confusion (do I want to identify with my Indian ancestry or identify with western ways, at least some of them) and the ubiquity of negative stereotypes of First Nations people. And there was no way I was going to let the doctors do that back operation they told me was risky. Don't they know there is such a thing as allowing time to heal naturally.*

And Canada is a country that is supposed to embrace the values of its people as a "Mosaic" as contrasted with the United States that has always embraced the virtues of the "Melting Pot". How did Indian people get left out of the Canadian Mosaic?

Kate found herself suddenly inspired. *What we need in this country is a "Mosaic Awareness Scale",* she thought. *A way to confront non-First Nations Canadians with their covert prejudices. They are not so prone to outright expression of discrimination now, with political correctness being the norm, but I can see it almost always on their faces. Is this person an Indian? Are they to be categorized as lazy, promiscuous, drunken, uncivilized, or even to be pitied, a classification I hate even more than lazy and unmotivated.*

"Hey Kate, whatever are you thinking about? You look like you are far off in a fog bank or something."

Kate managed a smile. It was another of the extras, Rory Broken Head, from the Plains Cree and Kate's Masters of Canadian History Program. *Most of the extras are Indians of course,* she mused, *while everyone else, the producer, the main actors, the technicians, and film crew are white. Even the fellow who supplied the oxen for the Red River carts is white.*

"We Indians are all like Rodney Dangerfield, Rory, remember, he complained that he didn't get any respect. Indians don't get any respect either. It's always been this way. Even in Grade Five I felt I had to prove somehow I was going to be more than the stereotypes that my teachers had of First Nations People. I've been overachieving ever since. I'm so tired. I need to slow down."

"So what's the use of dwelling on that? You know nothing is ever going to change. It's the Chicken House syndrome. We humans haven't got beyond ranking people yet. That must come from our Killer ape ancestors. We must have come from Chimpanzees not Bonobos. Bonobos look like small Chimpanzees but they don't get angry and kill each other like Chimpanzees do. The female Bonobos rule the roost and teach the young to use conflict resolution rather than violence to get their way."

"That's amazing." Kate was astonished at how smart Rory was. He was always demonstrating knowledge that she had never even thought about. "But what we need is a way of confronting the non-Indigenous Canadians about their covert and even sometimes overt, negative biases towards Indian people."

"How could you possibly do that? Every time we protest we get nothing but bad PR from the government and even the media. When Billy Diamond and the James Bay Cree in Quebec won the Supreme Court battle over unextinguished Indian title in the area they were going to flood for that huge hydro-electric project a massive public relations negative campaign was launched. Government and vested interests spent millions to paint First Nations people as getting vast sums of money they did and/or do not deserve.

Other resource multi-nationals and the current government have been using tactics like that ever since. Most Canadians

8

think First Nations' people are getting much more than ordinary Canadians. So much for legal rights we are supposed to have been given under Treaties. Fortunately the numbered treaties were done in such a haphazard manner, leaving the Chiefs of vast areas out of the negotiations, if you could call them that, we have been able to successfully win several huge land claims over the areas by way of arguing undistinguished Aboriginal title."

"We need a Mosaic Awareness Scale, Rory, a way to challenge non-Aboriginal Canadians about where they actually stand on the official version of what Canada is like, the perception that the Canadian Nation State is a Mosaic rather than A Melting Pot like the Americans. Heaven knows that our people have been under coercion to Assimilate ever since we were no longer needed as military allies for the British after the War of 1812 or workers or providers for the fur trade. Once the Hudson's Bay Company was given twenty percent of the arable land in the so-called fertile crescent of Rupert's Land as part of the settlement of its charter its officers then became more interested in settler land sales and development than furs."

"That treaty ending the War of 1812 was such a tragedy for all the tribes in the vast area in Indian Country below what became the border. For all of the American Revolution and again during the War of 1812 they supported Great Britain against France and the new American States only to be rewarded by total betrayal."

"I know. My grandmother, a Mohawk on the largest reserve in Canada, the one near Brantford Ontario, told me how our ancestors had first before the American Revolution been located in the vast area along the river systems below the St. Lawrence, the valleys of what are now Vermont, New York, Tennessee, and other American states. That was all supposed to remain neutral,

Indian Country. For most of the 18th. Century Sir William Johnson, the British Superintendent of Indian Affairs under George III, managed to use the Iroquois Federation and other tribes involved to maintain a balance of power between the land-hungry settlers of the Thirteen Colonies originally aligned with Great Britain and France and her colonies in Canada."

But when he died in5 1774 and the American Revolution started shortly after Sir William's descendants lacked the charm and diplomatic skills of their father. By the time the American Revolution ended Sir William's vast holdings in the Mohawk valley had been burned as well as myriads of farms in both the new country of America and the now British settlements in Upper Canada and around the St. Lawrence. An uneasy peace and the strength of the Iroquois Confederation were all that kept the land hungry Americans from driving out the re-maining tribes in Indian Country. In 1812 when the United States declared war on Great Britain, Canada was immediately invaded.

Many of the tribes of the Iroquois Confederation again sup-ported Britain and the horrible battles involving the American colonies and Great Britain for supremacy went on for several years. Chiefs like Tecumseh again saved key British forts from being defeated. Then the Treaty of Ghent to end the War of 1812 was negotiated. To the Iroquois Confederation and the other tribes in what was still called Indian Country an enormous betrayal by Great Britain for their loyalty of many decades oc-curred. The border was placed at the forty ninth parallell with the tribes all along the thirteen states placed at the mercy of the Americans. The Americans immediately started an Indian war to exterminate the tribes or force them to move west beyond the Mississippi.

That was when my great, great, great, great, great grandmother and many other tribesmen of the Iroquois Federation escaped to Canada. They moved to the Grand River, Ontario area where land had been put aside for the Iroquois because of their previous loyalty. The ones remaining in Indian Country below the border were forced to flee completely out of the area winding up in states like Oklahoma. So I think we need both a Mosaic Awareness scale as well as some way of getting the history known.

Kate felt Rory's piercing stare under his glasses. She could see him seriously considering what she had proposed.

"You know that's not a bad idea Kate. What would such a scale look like?"

Kate felt her depression lift. She felt some validation at last. Rory Broken Head was the brightest students in her Canadian History, Master's program. Kate thought fast. She had to come up with a prototype of the Mosaic Awareness Scale quickly if she was going to draw Rory to participate in its creation. She would need his understanding of statistics, questionnaire development and data collection.

"A scale of one to ten with weightings similar to those used for UFC Matches," she improvised.

"UFC Matches?"

"Ultimate Fight Challenges, you know the physical fights with almost anything allowed. That's what we are really in, Ultimate Fight Challenges to change the stereotypes of Canada's Indigenous people."

Kate watched Rory's facial expressions closely as she came up with the characteristics of the Mosaic Awareness Scale. Rory was a shy fellow. He seemed to come from his intellect rather than his heart which was unusual for First Nations people.

Kate improvised that the Mosaic Awareness Scale would challenge people to examine their conscious and unconscious attitudes towards First Nations people since contact. She told him that scoring as a Heavy Mosaic Weight (scores 7-8) would represent good understanding of Canada made up as a Mosaic with respect for distinct cultures including First Nations. At one end of the Scale, Super Heavy Mosaic Weight (scores nine to ten) could represent super awareness of the values in other's culture, and belief systems like in a true Mosaic.

"Fly Mosaic Weight (scores one to two) could represent Ethno-Centric Monoculturalism, the unconscious belief system that one's culture/religion/lifestyle are superior to all others."

"I like that," Kate's heart warmed as Rory praised her proposed scale. "Ethno-Centric Monoculturalism, the unconscious belief system of superiority of oneself and others like you, results in the extreme rigidity of forcing people to assimilate into the dominant belief system like your own. Can you believe it? Many of those people are well meaning as opposed to actual racists. Where can we put racists on the scale?"

"That would require a separate, Racist Scale. You have to have conscious beliefs to be a racist."

Kate continued to improvise the Mosaic Scale. She told Rory that Bantam Mosaic Weight, (scores three to four) could represent some fluidity in accepting other cultures value systems while Heavy Mosaic Weight (scores seven and eight) could represent a good level of fluidity in accepting that other's value systems have validity. She said that Light Heavy Mosaic Weight (scores five to six) could represent a moderate acceptance of other's value systems. Kate improvised that the other categories of the UFC could also be incorporated.

Katy suddenly found her heart racing as she realized that Rory had taken off his glasses and was giving her full eye contact indicating that he was intensely interested in her proposal. *Not again,* she repressed what she recognized as a sudden attraction to a member of the opposite sex. *He's good looking too,* some part of her mind warned her. *He's got issues,* it also warned. Katy was all too well aware that Rory's brother had committed suicide several years ago. She was jolted back from alarms going off in her system by Rory's handsomeness and his intense interest in her proposal.

Watch out, some part of Kate's mind warned her. *There you go again. Remember, this fellow is not like most First Nations people. He closed down his feelings when his brother died. He comes from his intellect and is not emotionally available. He thinks using an analytic mind rather than an open heart is the way to go. As your favorite Indian author, Vine Deloria Jr., said in the book "The Vine DeLoria Reader" we need to question the positions of many, university authorities as their unquestioned conclusions about Indigenous peoples are often only the result of peer hypothesis and consensus.*

Kate chuckled as she recalled Deloria's hilarious criticisms of Anthropologists claims that Paleo-Indians had pursued the large mammals such as the Wooly Mammoth over the hypothesized Bering Land Bridge and were responsible for their extinction using Clovis- tipped arrowheads. Rory is much too accepting of authority figures in his university.

"You know Kate that there needs to be a timeline involved in this scale. People think that attitudes towards First Nations' people have changed in the over four hundred years since contact but have they really. First Nations' people have been under constant expectation of first, extermination, then Assimilation, particularly after the War of 1812 and ever since we lost our valued position as military allies, geographical guides, pemmican suppliers and workforce for the fur trade."

"How would you incorporate a timeline?"

"A Series of Quilt-Like Structure" Rory improvised. "Each quilt with squares of various sizes showing the influence of Canada's dominant world views and belief systems at points in time. For instance, just after Contact by John Cabot, 1550 to 1600. The large square quilt would be divided into only three panels, say a large, yellow square representing the Dominant world view in Northern, North America at that time, that of the hunter-gatherer tribes in rugged areas of the northern continent above the 49th. Parallel that didn't support agriculture.

Kate had to process with her mind as Rory elaborated further. She listened carefully as he told her that an off-yellow square could represent the belief system of the Iroquois Confederation that had developed fortified villages with palisades and agricultural production before the French Colonialists arrived. Rory said that another, slightly brownish square could represent the sophistication of the western, coastal tribes of what is now British Columbia. Rory told her that the British Columbia First Nations had developed elaborate art and living conditions because of the plentiful food supply and beneficial weather available to them.

He added that only a small blue square would represent the influence of the Euro-Centric belief system of explorers such as Cabot and perhaps another small silver square could represent the belief systems of people like the Vikings who had established small settlements for a time.

"Look, I'll draw some squares in the dirt here."

Kate watched in fascination as Rory picked up a sharp stick and began drawing quilts in the sand.

"See, here's pre-contact. Several large colored squares represent Indian values of the many different tribes. Despite European's conviction that Indians lacked any semblance of religious beliefs all the tribes believed and many still believe in a Creator God and a system of natural laws that regulated interactions of humans with other species and forms of life on the planet. The tiny square represents Viking values in the brief occupations from Vikings in Labrador. It could be colored silver. Anthropologists now think that Vikings interacted with the Indigenous people here. Their world view certainly included that it was right to trespass and conquer. A tiny sliver colored pink might represent possible belief systems from contacts from possible encounters with other sea-faring peoples via the Pacific or Atlantic oceans."

Kate concentrated as Rory elaborated further. He told her that another quilt could represent 1600 t0 1650.

"People in Canada don't realize the huge battles that went on between the European Nations vying for world domination, particularly Britain and France although Spain, Russia, Holland and Portugal also got in on the action. Europeans had already used up the wood from their own forests, overfished, polluted their rivers, developed agriculture and animal husbandry and now had surplus populations they did not know what to do with. After England had defeated Spain there were many left-over conquistadors and other desperados without work or land. They were sent to South America and were busy laying waste to the Indigenous populations of the Caribbean and South America. Christopher Columbus had led the way to the Americas.

In 1600 with Imperialistic World Views, Britain and France's rulers sent soldiers and warships to exploit the new world and placed clergy and settlers amongst the myriads of tribes that rightfully occupied what became Canada and the United States in order to justify their takeover of the lands and resources. They developed theories that as the occupants were not Christian the lands could be considered uninhabited. Their value system that agricultural production was superior to hunting/gathering was used to pronounce the Indians ownership of land as non-productive and subject to take-over. They of course did not notice that the vast grasslands of the prairies had been gradually developed by Indigenous people burning grasses in the fall to support growing populations of buffalo and antelope that provided their food sources."

Kate listened closely comparing her own knowledge about the early time eras to Rory's. She agreed with him when he related that in 1605 the French established a settlement at Port Royal in what is now Nova Scotia. In 1607 England established its first settlement at Virginia while in 1608 Samuel de Champlain established a settlement at Quebec for France.

"It wasn't long before settlers in what would become the United States wanted the lands of the French for expansion. In 1613 under the Governor of Virginia, Sir Thomas Dale, a force of mercenaries drove the French settlers out of Acadia. The Acadians eventually returned but the terrible battles between England and France kept occurring with great frequency."

Kate listened closely as Rory related that in 1690 soldiers came from Massachusetts, enabled by thirty-four ships from New York. Over twenty-three hundred men attacked Quebec but Frontenac refused to surrender and with Huron help the troops were forced to retreat. In 1690 Rory related how the British joined forces with American Colonists to try and gain the fertile areas around the St. Lawrence. Forty-five ships with six thousand, five hundred men moved on Quebec while two thousand, three hundred troops advanced towards Montreal via

Lake Champlain but met a huge storm in the St. Lawrence and withdrew. In 1713 as a result of treaties, Acadia (Nova Scotia) was ceded back to Britain.

"What about the quilt patterns. What does that say about the World Views at that time?"

"Right, the Yellow Square of the world view of tribes such as the Hurons who aided the French and the Purple Iroquois Confederation Square, whose warriors aided the British, remained large because of the necessity of the settlers relying on the Indians for food, as guides, and as military allies. The French Green square and the British Red square grew larger as the great powers aided their settlements in the areas by sending more soldiers, warships and supplies. France and England were actually battling for supremacy in the world by using their colonies for the battles just like the Japanese and the Americans fought most of World War II in the South Pacific. The English and French squares continued to expand and contract, though, with attacks, wars and negotiations."

"What was behind the terrible battles of the Europeans for more territory, Rory?" Kate had always wondered why western civilization was so full of wars and violence.

"Remember the Chimpanzees and Bonobos, Kate? We most likely came from the Chimpanzees."

Kate found herself laughing.

"But really Europeans have always been incredible polluters and wasters of resources. Their development of agriculture and animal husbandry had been the means of the incredible population explosion in Europe. By even the early fifteen hundreds Europeans had used up most of their forests for heating, lodging, castles and weapons like ewe bows. They had also polluted their rivers, overfished, and had these huge populations of peasants, soldiers and religious heretics they needed to do something with. The rulers of Spain, England, France, Portugal, Holland were happy to send them overseas to the new lands that awaited exploitation."

"So while the large Yellow Square of the tribes such as the Hurons who aided the French and Purple Square of the Iroquois Confederation who aided the English remained strong, French and British squares grew and diminished in what would become both Canada and the United States as battles both in Europe and in North America and the subsequent peace treaties altered their possessions."

Kate continued to compare her knowledge to that of Rory as he moved the timeline of Canadian history from 1711 to 1755. He related that by the end of that time period the colored squares in the quilt pattern would have shifted completely.

Rory reported that in 1720 the French built a trading post at Niagara across Lake Ontario. In 1721 the British built Fort Oswego. In 1754 the French and Indian War started. Rory added that in the 1750's twenty thousand French Acadians occupied Nova Scotia. Kate flinched as Rory recalled that in 1755 all Acadians were expelled and the Abnaki Indians were driven from the land to be replaced by New England settlers from what would become the United States of America. In 1755 Sir William Johnson became a British national hero when he and the Iroquois Confederation of tribes he had managed to make himself acceptable to fought off an attack by French Commander Van Dieskau at Lake George. He was rewarded with a Baronet and appointed Superintendent of Indians.

"Things got worse when England declared war on France in 1756. The American colonies wanted the vast Ohio-Mississippi valleys that were in Indian and French voyageur fur trader's hands. The French used alliances with the Hurons and guerilla warfare to resist. This prompted the Pennsylvania governor to place a bounty of one hundred thirty Spanish dollars for the scalp of every male enemy Indian and fifty dollars for females."

Kate felt much pain for her Indian ancestors as Rory related that in 1756 the struggle for world supremacy between Britain and France resulted in twenty one thousand blue uniformed American colonists attacking New France. In July 1759 Louisburg fell and in the Ohio Valley, Fort Duquesne fell and was renamed Pittsburg. In June of 1759 one thousand four hundred French settler farms were burned by the British near the Plains of Abraham.

"That's when New France's ally, Chief Pontiac of the Ottawas in 1763 allied with the Ojibwa and Potawatomi and drove back the American and English settlers in the region south of the Great Lakes. That vast region was not given to the American colonies upon settlement of the war and became for a while a neutral Indian territory.

By the Proclamation of 1763 New France was dismembered and renamed the Province of Quebec. Labrador was annexed to Newfoundland and Prince Edward Island and Cape Breton handed to Nova Scotia.

"There is now a much reduced yellow square representing the influence of First Nations People who have been largely displaced in the Maritimes by Euro-Centric settlers but remain strong, if somewhat changed by the influence of the fur trade, in the Plains and Northern areas. Britain has conquered French colonies at Quebec and Montreal with the aid of the Iroquois. The English King has assigned all the land in what would become Prince Edward Island to his cronies in the British Aristocracy leaving nothing to the Mi'kmacs there. Mainly British settlers have settled Upper Canada and a British square in the quilt now becomes a large red square of influence.

A green square represents the thought patterns of the remaining, conquered, French settlers in Lower Canada. Although the British had won Quebec they needed the help of the remaining French settlers to keep the colony going. As a result much of the French legal and business system of combining the Catholic Church and state was allowed to continue. A black square can represent the thought patterns of the many Americans who have already come to Canada."

Kate listened carefully as Rory jumped further ahead in time. He told Kate that after 1763 we would have another drastic change to the quilt patterns. He related that George III has issued the Proclamation that now required public meetings to be held and treaties to be signed to extinguish native rights to lands west of what is now Ontario. The King had been alarmed at the direct, individual buying by American settlers of land from tribes and wanted to keep the privilege of purchasing Indian lands strictly to the Crown whose representatives would now distribute it.

"The Red Square of British, Imperialistic thought becomes even larger. And now we add an Orange Square, the start of the thought patterns of the settler population who would before long become Canadian, bent on making their lives for themselves and their families better than it would have been from where they have come from. To them the First Nations people were only an impediment to be eliminated. An era of White Supremacy was added at this time with the Myth of the white Superior race, so-called superior civilization because of agriculture, animal husbandry, and the unquestioned supremacy of the Christian religion. The proclamation itself will cause great problems for land claim negotiations in the twenty-first century and beyond."

"The unrest in the American colonies added even more confusion," Kate felt herself contributing. "Now French speaking settlers in Quebec and Montreal, Scottish settlers and British regulars would find themselves fighting alongside the Iroquois Six Nation Confederation to defend Canada from invasion from the South. In a mind-boggling turn of events France would now be allied with America in its War of Independence."

"Then it got even worse for Britain's Indian allies. The American Colonies were determined to grab all of Canada and particularly the vast, supposedly Neutral Indian Country along the Ohio and Mississippi River systems for their Empire. They wanted Canada as a Fourteenth State."

"Yes," Kate listened in agreement as Rory continued. Twelve hundred men under General Benedict Arnold invaded Canada from Maine while General Montgomery marched in November, 1775 towards Montreal with eight thousand troops. Montreal fell but because of an Indian messenger warning of the coming attack on Quebec and Governor Carleton's escape from Montreal and his reorganization of French Canadian, British, Scottish and Newfoundland troops, Quebec was not conquered. In Dec. 31, 1775 half of the American forces were captured killed or wounded.

Six thousand more troops came up from America but British troops arrived at Quebec and along with Indian allies saved the day. As historian David Orchard, in his book "The Fight for Canada" says "Without the loyalty of the French Canadians there would not be today an acre of land above the 49th. parallel without the Stars and Stripes flying." That statement should have also included the loyalty of the Iroquois Confederation along the St. Lawrence, and below the Great Lakes in the Mohawk, Ohio and Mississippi valleys.

"However," Kate winced as Rory continued, "so-called diplomacy again resulted in areas being given to America that had been administered from Canada for one hundred years or had been previously declared neutral Indian Country. The territory between the Ohio and Mississippi rivers which would become Michigan, Wisconsin, Illinois, Ohio and Indiana as well as most of the Great Lakes were given to the U.S. under the Treaty of Paris in 1783."

Kate felt great pain as Rory recounted how the lands of the Six Nations, despite Mohawk Chief Joseph Brant's unswerving loyalty to the British in the Mohawk Valley, promised to him by the King of England, were given to New York.

Kate was fascinated by Rory's quilt patterns and watched with great intensity as he started to draw another. However they were interrupted by a loud voice.

"Who's your friend Rory?" Kate turned to find a tall, strikingly handsome, man in a business suit.

Chapter 2. Documentary Expansion.

George McBay, the CEO of the film company, found himself staring unexpectedly at the young, First Nations woman that his acquaintance Rory Broken Head was sitting beside. He could feel his body react to her beauty.

Wow, some part of his mind told him. *She's gorgeous, exotic and young, just what you've been looking for. That lovely lady is just the kind of woman that turns you on.*

"Oh, Mr. McBay welcome to the film shoot. This is my classmate, Kate Golden Eagle. She's one of the extras for the documentary. Kate, this is our producer. What are you doing here Mr. McBay? I thought you were back in Vancouver taking care of funding."

Kate felt a body response as the youngish Producer grasped her hand warmly and beamed at her.

"So pleased to make your acquaintance, Kate."

He's holding your hand longer than he should, some part of Kate's mind warned her.

"The pleasure is mutual," she managed.

"Rory, I need you to come back to Vancouver with me. I've almost got my father to agree to finance a series rather than just this one documentary, but I need more help on the history end. My father needs convincing that there's enough drama to keep people interested in a complete TV series. I thought of you immediately after our discussions at the start of this shoot. You've been studying Canadian History for years, right?"

"Yes. So has Kate. We're both about to finish a Master's Degree in Canadian History."

The lady is intelligent, some part of George McBay's mind alerted him. *You always like your lovers tall, beautiful, exotic and smart.*

"My major is First Nations History," Kate tried to explain. She could feel the producer's piercing gaze going over her as he took in that information.

Watch out, some part of Katy's mind warned her. *He's really handsome too,* it added. Kate could feel her heart reacting as she took in the producer's superb build. *Well, I shouldn't have to worry about getting too close to him,* she decided. *I bet he only dates advantaged women of his social class.* Katy found herself scanning his left hand. No wedding ring was apparent.

Take her back to Vancouver with you, some part of George McBay's mind ordered. *You could even promise to make her a big star. Promise to feature her in the film or series somehow. Get to know her intimately. She's the type you always look for, gorgeous, exotic and vulnerable. And an Indian Princess lover would send your father right over the edge. How nice it would be to get back at him. He's always loved your younger brother more than you.*

George McBay felt adrenaline flowing through his veins. *She would be a challenge,* his mind told him *but you always prefer a challenge, as long as you win of course.*

You don't like people telling you what to do, another part of George's mind argued, *this women has spirit.* George could feel the anger that he knew came from his overbearing father forever telling him what to do. *You never listen anyway, some part of his mind argued back.* George let his usual impulsivity take over as he made an instant decision.

"Look, I've just had a brainwave. I need both of you to come with me. It will likely take more than one Canadian History expert to convince my father that Canadian History is not as boring as he thinks it is. I've got a helicopter idling at the end of the cart procession. Grab some clothes. I need to get both of you back to Vancouver before my father leaves for the States. If we could tackle this project as a series instead of a single documentary we could save having to shoot many of the locations over again. We might even be able to sell the finished product as a TV series."

"What about the shoot. We're scheduled to start filming in a few days?"

"Don't worry. You're just extras. You can be replaced. I need Canadian history experts right now. And Kate, that's you name right, is extremely beautiful, don't you think Rory. I've had another brainwave. I think I will be able to feature her as a star in the documentary. I'll transfer you and quadruple whatever your salary is, both of you. I shouldn't tell you this but this documentary is my chance to make it big. My father has finally financed one of my projects instead of my brothers. He's finally letting me do a project I want to do instead of me forever being ordered to do projects of his choice. I'll wait for both of you in the helicopter."

Kate stared at Rory in complete alarm as their producer hurried back towards the end of the cart procession. She could see by Rory's eyes that he was in deep thought.

"So does that man have brainwaves every five minutes? I'm a History major not an actress. Whatever is he thinking?"

"Kate, this might be a great opportunity for us. Maybe we can both finance a Ph.D. if George McBay finds he really needs us. But watch out for him. He's known as a notorious womanizer and he was giving you a close going over. Just make sure you don't encourage him to get closer."

Not again, some part of Katie's mind warned her. *You think both of these fellows are possible future soul mates. Nothing could be further from their minds. You look like a grown-up woman but part of you is emotionally immature. Particularly about relationships. Those Hollywood, romance movies you used to watch and the romantic novels you read to escape the pain of feeling you were not good enough makes you vulnerable to romantic fantasies. You've been brainwashed by the movie industry.*

Kate intuitively felt some truth in the accusations. *I must have read every romantic novel published from when I was eleven to sixteen,* she acknowledged. *But that handsome guy did give me a thorough, piercing look. And he isn't married.*

"Surely, George McBay only dates advantaged women, women in the same social class as himself."

"Men like him marry only advantaged women. They date others for obvious reasons. I've heard lots of gossip about Mr. McBay."

"Gossip?"

"Some say that he dates non-white women just to get back at his racist father."

"Why would he do that?"

"His younger brother was made CEO of his father's company rather than him."

"Rory! You want me to associate with someone who is obsessed with non-white women! That sounds extremely masochistic. And what about the Mosaic Awareness Scale and the Quilt Project?"

"That's what I'm talking about Kate. This opportunity might give us the money to keep working on them. Maybe if we can save enough money we can go right into a Ph.D. project instead of finishing our Masters and use the Mosaic Awareness Scale and the Quilt Project for a joint dissertation topic. Or maybe we can incorporate those concepts into the series, if Mr. McBay gets the funding for the project."

"You think the Mosaic Awareness Scale is that important?"

"I think it's absolutely brilliant."

Kate could feel a very warm feeling around her heart. *Rory is noticing you for the first time,* some part of Kate's mind told her. *You are making the same mistakes again,* another part of Kate's mind warned her.

Nonsense, Rory's right. Kate decided to go along with Rory and take George McBay up on his offer. *He just wants Canadian History experts. Rory and I are certainly that. I don't know about the actress part but at least I can give my back a rest from the ox-cart ride,* she sighed. *Maybe I can save it from flaring further and having to undergo the back surgery my doctor wants me to have done. And not only that I'll be with Rory. We'll have to work closely together. Maybe this is a chance to get to know him much better.* Kate stared at her ox cart and realized she was likely being saved from further back injury.

"All right I'll come but you had better make sure I'm never alone with that Producer."

The next morning Kate Golden Eagle found herself staring out the window at the magnificent view of the Vancouver Harbor she could see from Geoge McBay's luxurious three bedroom apartment. He had brought Rory and Kate directly to his place from the airport when the helicopter had touched down. She and Rory had stayed the night as his guests. She sat down on one of the red, leather chesterfields in the living/dining room as George McBay called them away from the breakfast table to convene.

"Rory tells me you are a distant relative of Chief Keenoshayoo, the chief negotiator for Treaty 8," Kate was amazed to be queried. She felt completely out of place in her worn jeans and cotton shirt in the luxurious surroundings.

Here you go again, some part of her mind warned. *Having to prove yourself to a white, authority figure. Just do it. Turn up your power chakra.*

"I am," she admitted. "Chief Keenoshayoo was a distant cousin of my great, great, great, great, great, great, grandfather. He was a Woods Cree but had taken a Mohawk woman as his wife."

"Then we have a lot in common," George McBay's voice turned humorous. "My great, great, great, great. great, grandfather was distantly related to the Honorable David Laird, the chief negotiator for the government of Canada in Treaty 8."

"It really is a small world," Kate managed.

"To be honest with you, the reason my father is financing my documentary is to show what a great job his distant relative did in negotiating Treaty 8 in 1899. That Treaty extinguished the title of a vast territory known as Rupert's Land and secured such valuable areas as the present Tar Sands Development in Northern Alberta and the gold in the Yukon for the Dominion of Canada."

Alarms went off in Kate's mind at George McBay's words. She had for all of her graduate program been trying to make sense of the history of the policies towards Canada's Indigenous people carried out first by the French and Great Britain administrators and then by Canadian administrators once the British North America Act created the Dominion of Canada in 1867.

She did not agree at all with what George McBay was saying. She looked at Rory to correct their boss. She expected him to set the record straight but was shocked when he told her with his eyes and facial expression just to go along with what she was hearing without protest.

Kate quickly went over in her mind what she knew about Treaty 8. She was indeed a distant descendent of Chief Keenoshayoo. The Chief had been the chief negotiator for Objibwa and Cree natives who had signed, or at least had made copies of their totems in front of witnesses, to the infamous Treaty 8 that had surrendered most of the land of an immense territory in 1899. Rupert's Land had stretched westward all the way from Lesser Slave Lake near Hudson Bay, across Northern and Central Alberta, Saskatchewan, Manitoba, part of British Columbia, the Northwest Territories, the Yukon and down to slightly north of present day Edmonton, Regina and Winnipeg.

Title to Rupert's Land was surrendered in return for promises that gave hope to First Nation's people being invaded by epidemics, starvation, settlers, remorseless fire water traders and when gold was discovered in Barkerville and the Klondike, as James Douglass called them in B.C., the "rowdies" of the world. Many of the "rowdies" came from the United States and had no respect for the people who had occupied the territory for centuries.

On their way to Yukon gold, the "rowdies" often killed the native's horses, shot their dogs and broke up their bear traps. Seeking the B.C. gold in the Fraser River would-be miners often shot natives on sight. American Whiskey traders had moved into the Plains and pedaled firewater for the buffalo robes, the live buffalo sources of which were being rapidly extinguished due to the repeater rifle and the demand for buffalo hide to be made into conveyer belts on the new machinery of the Industrial Age.

In the United States both the Native's two major sources of food, the buffalo and the Passenger Pigeon were being exterminated by bounty hunters. The U.S. government was determined to deliberately exterminate the Natives food supplies. In one year alone a billion Passenger Pigeons were shot, clubbed or burned alive in trees while the buffalo were almost wiped from the face of the earth.

Other furs that had kept the Indians in what had become necessary goods from the Hudson's Bay trading forts were now in 1899 also diminishing rapidly from over trapping from competing American fur traders moving into Canada. The First Nations people of the Plains and further north were realizing that the white men invading their territory were eager to latch onto the minerals and other valuable commodities they were noticing in their lands, not to mention the land itself.

Kate suppressed her back pain that the tension induced and repressed a grimace as her new boss, the handsome George McBay, a descendent of the Honorable David Laird, the very person who had helped negotiate Treaty 7 and particularly Treaty 8 in the late 1800's, sat down opposite Rory and her. Some part of her mind was telling her that he was the possible soul mate that she had been waiting for while another part was telling her that even if he was interested in a romantic liaison a serious problem would happen between them because of George McBay's and/ or his father's obvious pride at their distant relative's success at disinheriting Indians through Treaties. The more Kate read of Canadian history the more she was becoming aware of the terrible consequences for her people of their own distant ancestor's actions.

Kate found her emotions going out of control and Sciatica pain striking again. The knowledge about the incredible cruelty to Indian children because of Treaty 8's confinement of Plains and Northern Indians to reserves and the subsequent banishment of the children to Residential Schools was triggering both her back problem and her emotions. The pain of two failed love affairs was also greatly amplifying her emotions. She found herself trying to get through to George McBay how David Laird's Treaty 7 and 8 had started the complete subjugation of the Plains people.

"Look Mr. McBay, I'm not sure I can participate in a project designed to show David Laird as a hero. Treaty 8 was designed to as cheaply as possible limit the threat to the flood of incoming settlers that the new Dominion of Canada would bring in by completing the subjugation of the Plains Indians and those Indians further north that started with Treaty 7." Kate ignored Rory's look of horror.

"We'll negotiate," Kate was amazed at George McBay's words. "Tell me what you think really happened back then. I'm not sure it matters much now anyways with Canada almost fully occupied by non-Aboriginal people."

Kate felt herself losing total emotional control. She found herself lecturing George McBay and totally ignoring Rory's frantic hand signals behind George McBay's back to tone things down.

"Your ancestor David Laird followed John A. MacDonald's orders to arrange surrender of Rupert's Land at the least possible cost. Eliminated in Treaties 7 and 8 were the clauses for famine and epidemic protection contained in Treaty 6 negotiated by his predecessor, Lieutenant Governor Morris, who had been forced to deal with Chiefs who could already see the end of the Bison and the coming of epidemics amongst their people."

See I told you she would argue with you, George McBay found some part of his mind gloating.

I like a challenge, he argued back. *I'll just let her words flow over me. She looks really beautiful when she gets intense.* George sat back and thought about financial funding as he let Kate's words go unprocessed.

"First Nations chiefs had thought they were negotiating Nation to Nation treaties with honorable people who would share the resources of their lands with them. Actually when David Laird negotiated Treaty 8, the Indian Act had already been passed. The Indian Act would condemn Indians to be treated like children, wards of the state under Indian Agents from whom there would be no way to appeal. They would now be told where to live, how to govern their bands, what they could and could not do and how much resources they would be given or not given to even survive the epidemics and starvation coming their way."

George's mind came back to the present as Kate's voice stopped.

"Do you realize how photogenic you get when you get emotional? And your voice. Star quality for sure, with a few lessons from a professional coach! Don't you think so Rory?" Kate felt her emotions surge even more.

"Uh, I guess you are right Mr. McBay. Kate does look extremely photogenic when she gets intense."

He's not listening to you at all, some part of her mind warned. He just sees you as a pretty face, and a body. And what's wrong with Rory? He's not even trying to set the record straight. Kate's emotions flared and she tried again to get through to her boss.

"Your ancestor, David Laird of course made no mention of the Indian Act and let the Chiefs believe that their people would be given assistance with medicine in time of epidemics and food rations in time of famine even though those clauses from Treaty 6 had been already removed for Treaties 7 and 8. Of course he didn't tell them that. The Chiefs signing Treaty 8 were given assurances that their prized mobility, their freedom to hunt and gather, the heart of their culture and religion, would still be intact while the reality was that planners in Ottawa were deciding to restrict Indians to reserves without freedom to move out of them and under control of Indian Agents."

Kate winced as George McBay ignored what she had said and continued on without seemingly paying any attention at all to her words.

"I'm hoping that the documentary will be accepted for the prestigious Toronto Film Festival in 2017, the one hundred and fiftieth anniversary of the Dominion of Canada," he explained. "But Rory here has convinced me that we have enough material for a series. I need both of you to help me convince my father to fund the series."

I should have remained an extra, Katy mused. *To most white people's minds the older Indian woman has always only been an extra, a largely invisible form inside a tipi taking care of what they have always regarded as uncivilized, rudimentary, food-related tasks and young children. Or to many white men, the Indian woman was fantasized as an Indian Princess.* Pictures from the myriads of postcards used in the nineteen tens, nineteen twenties and nineteen thirties to lure first settlers and then tourists poured into Kate's mind. *Caucasian-looking, young females dressed in buckskins and beads, all alone, paddling a birch-bark canoe and looking wistfully for their romantic white man,* Kate thought.

It's worse than that, some part of Kate's mind kicked in. *Once the settlers flooded the Plains from 1867 on Indian women were regarded by white society as having deplorable morals. Under the Indian Act, they and their children lost Indian status permanently when they married a white man and Indian women had to prove they were of worthy character even to receive an inheritance from their own father.*

That stereotype, the subordinate, promiscuous, young Indian woman, still exists today in the minds of many low morality white men and is likely partially if not wholly to blame for the trail of disappeared and murdered Aboriginal women across Canada and the failure to quickly and thoroughly investigate their deaths. *When Canadians and particularly Americans think of Indians of the past they automatically think of the men as warriors attacking worthy hordes of settlers in wagon trains crossing the west, and of the women as exotic Indian Princesses falling for a handsome white man thanks to the movie industry and movies like Pocahontas.*

Kate managed to dig her fingernails into her hands to repress her surging emotions. Her psychic pain was enormous. *If only I'd remained one of the extras I could have returned quickly to finish my M.A.* Kate repressed another emotional outburst. *Now I'm getting in this over my head. And these men are both much too attractive. That part of my mind that tells me I am still vulnerable to looks is absolutely right.*

Despite forebodings, Kate felt her body respond to her boss's sensuous voice, luxurious surroundings and attractive facade. She forced herself to ignore the sensation and concentrate on the task at hand.

"What parts of Canadian history could be expected to be dramatic enough to interest film audiences?"

Kate felt a powerful emotional surge, sensed an opportunity and found herself trying to educate her boss again.

"Can you believe it, a million acres of the best agricultural land exchanged for twenty-five thousand acres of poor land on Manitoulin Island?"

"Here?"

"No, back in what is now Ontario. Iroquois people had been given land around the Grand River after First Nations people of the Iroquois Six Nations fought for the British in the War of 1812. The Iroquois blocked the American soldiers from entering through the Niagara Valley. Once that series of horrendous battles was over the Natives were not valuable anymore. We were not needed militarily and our title had to be extinguished in order to make way for the myriads of settlers who were needed to guarantee British ownership of the rapidly expanding colonies of Upper and Lower Canada."

"That's just ancient history. My father says that you natives just need to get over your obsession with Colonialism."

Kate felt complete fury going through her veins. She glared at Rory but his eyes and hand motions just beseeched her to tone down her remarks.

"No. It's really ironic. There wouldn't even be a Canada if our people had not fought for Great Britain against the French, against the Americans during their Revolution and particularly the War of 1812. Both Indians and settlers would likely have become Americans. After the War of 1812 Iroquois people who moved to Canada and other tribes were supposed to become farmers instead of primarily hunters/gatherers but we were to do it on an island with poor agricultural potential. Sir Francis Bond Head, the new English Governor in charge of Canada wanted the Iroquois Confederation people to move from the land we had been allowed to settle, the Grant around the Grand River near Kitchener to Manitoulin Island and grow crops on rocks. And the Iroquois who had fought with the British in Indian Country below the border that now became the Eastern U.S. were left to the mercy of the American Calvary."

You had better let this lady think you are open to her views on Indigenous history, some part of George McBay's mind warned him.

She's getting really angry and she might just walk out the door. George acknowledged the warning.

"Tell me about that. If what you say is true maybe we should try and expand this documentary to include the earlier treaties."

Kate blinked. George McBay seemed to be listening. She really wanted to get back to her history studies at the University of Calgary. She wanted to finish them and enter Law school before she was twenty-five. Now she was becoming bogged down in a past that filled her with despair and could sense she was being attracted to men who were both emotionally unavailable as had been her other two lovers.

"The story doesn't even start there," Kate felt even more depression. "It starts back on the Eastern sea coast. The Beothuks of Newfoundland were the first to go. They were quickly driven inland by the power of the guns of the fisherman of just about every European nation. The fishermen came to plunder the flourishing cod fisheries off the island. Then, the timber and seals of Nova Scotia and New Brunswick were coveted. Europeans severely disrupted the hunting and gathering patterns of First Nations people in the Maritimes.

And eventually harassment if not outright genocide of the Beothuks took place as they moved inland from the sea and their fisheries as small European settlements began, originally to dry and salt the fish for transport. Then the settlers arrived. The Beothuks had always survived by fishing in the summer and in the fall on whatever game they could find in the inhospitable interior of what is now Newfoundland. This pattern was interrupted and they gradually weakened from starvation and disease as well as being deliberately shot by the fishermen and settlers until the natives were totally wiped out."

"What about Prince Edward Island?"

"Can you believe it? The Mi'kmaq people were not even considered when Prince Edward Island was divided into huge lots and given to members of the British Aristocracy by the King in 1750. If the Aboriginal Protection Society of Great Britain had not purchased Lennox Island there would be no Mi'kmaq in Prince Edward Island today nor Maliseet in Nova Scotia where they kept being relocated to land that was virtually useless at that time."

"But look what replaced them in Nova Scotia. Halifax became the world's capital for the building of magnificent sailing ships. As my father says, progress was inevitable. What about further West?"

Kate forced herself to ignore her boss's lack of compassion for the fate of the Beothuks and other First Nations people in Nova Scotia, New Brunswick and Prince Edward Island. She tried again to educate him.

"The lands of the Huron and Iroquois were plundered first with settlement from the French in the sixteen hundreds and the English in the seventeen hundreds. The Huron aligned with the French who practiced gift diplomacy. The Iroquois aligned with the lesser of what they viewed as the two evils, the British, as the two European nations fought for supremacy along the St. Lawrence River systems. Without the Iroquois the British would likely never have conquered Quebec, or stopped the Americans from invading during the Revolutionary War and in the War of 1812 using both the warriors of the Iroquois Confederation and other tribes.

"But look what eventually came out of that, the great country of Canada. Would you rather have become American?"

Kate grimaced. She felt like her mind was turning to mush, her back pain was flaring and a sharp pain struck her heart. There seemed to be no way to get her boss and to see the other side of the story. The demise of huge, flourishing civilizations that managed to survive in a challenging, natural world for hundreds if not thousands of years. A culture that respected animals and even plants as valued creations of the Great Spirit and requested their agreement before sacrificing their life to humans. Only what was needed as food was taken, no more.

People like him still believe the Myth of empty North and South American continents before 1492, Kate mused.

"Look Mr. McBay. It's a myth that the Indigenous people who lived in North and South America were at a lesser stage of civilization than Europeans at 1492 because they did not develop the agriculture or animal husbandry with domesticated animals that allowed the huge population expansion of Europe. Actually great civilizations flourished in both North and South America. The Incas occupied two thousand miles on the West Coast of South America, fed by an agricultural development concerning terrace growing of various types of potatoes. At one time one hundred million people were fed. Llamas and Alpacas were domesticated contributing wool and meat. In the Amazon, land that has now returned to jungle, one hundred square kilometers had been agriculturally domesticated.

In North America around 1150 A.D., people known as the Mississippians had become farmers, developing strains of corn from what had been tiny wild ones into crops that fed thousands of people. In the prairies native peoples had developed the periodic burning of the grasslands that expanded them resulting in twenty million square kilometers becoming pastures for the thirty million Bison that became a food supply for an expanding population. Fishing on coasts of both continents supplied many native peoples with abundance.

"Isn't that irrelevant? Those civilizations disappeared anyway."

"They disappeared from diseases. Smallpox and other diseases after contact resulted in ninety percent of Indigenous people in the America's dying."

"My father would say that was a sign from God that the land was being cleared for European occupation."

"You don't understand" Kate's anger broke out again. "The French were the first to label our people *sauvage and sauvagess*. They could not comprehend the real nature of the Iroquois and Huron civilization they happened upon trying to find a route to the riches of the Orient. Our people were communal. Our families loved one another, even extended families. We supported each other. We believed in a higher power governing all living things. We honored the animals, taking only what we needed to survive. We had no need of the minerals and resources the French and the British found so valuable. Our movement throughout the great continent of North America before European contact, in summer to hunt and gather, in winter to give thanks to the Great Spirit for his beneficence, barely left a trace on the natural world."

"What about all those furs that the natives exchanged with the fur traders and what about the battles between the different tribes."

"That came mainly later. After our people were dazzled by the muskets and cannon of the invaders and encouraged into consumer goods by the traders, particularly the liquor traders, the alcohol of which our people had no immunity. It was the Europeans who interrupted their natural way of life. Before guns and metal tools natives spent most of their time gathering, hunting and processing resources to make it through the winters. We did not have time for the massive battles the French, British and later the Americans fought as part of their Imperialistic, world view. Before contact only the odd raid occurred as different tribes encountered one another in their different territories."

"Then we come to the eighteen and nineteen hundreds. All across this vast country, second only in size to that of the U.S.S.R. before it imploded, treaties were done to remove Indian Nations from their lands. That's what the early Peace and Friendship and the Numbered Treaties one to eleven were all about. The Huron, Iroquois, Woods Cree, the Plains Cree, the Blackfoot, Chipewyan's, the Dogrib, the Inuit, the Dene, the Ojibwa, and all the others lost their lands and their way of life."

"That happened way back then. It was the same all over the world. Out of that came modern civilization. Would you rather be living in a tipi? After all reserves were set in place and schools."

Kate's amygdala fired again. Her body tensed and she could feel her Sciatica Nerve attacking her left leg.

"The Infamous Residential Schools! You think that was progress for my people. Those schools represent incredible cruelty to the children. Fifty percent of those children never returned home. They died because of inadequate food and infections that could have been prevented. The rest were removed from parents, indoctrinated instead of educated, and spent most of their lives with incredible low self-worth from experiencing physical, emotional and/or sexual abuse and put-downs because of their being Indians. They were regarded as subhuman by most of their indoctrinators and often predatory teachers and authority figures."

"That's better than the superstitious belief systems Indians lived under. Some of those students even went on to higher education." Kate could feel herself losing it completely.

"Look Mr. McBay, what we have here for this documentary is a culture clash of massive proportions. The pre-contact cultures and belief systems of what are now the First Nations people of Canada, Non-Status Indians and Urban Indians could not be totally wiped out. They collided with the white supremacy belief systems of Europeans and still do. Cruel methods of starvation, incarceration and indoctrination did not succeed in their task of removing Indian belief systems. They just produced incredible identity achievement problems that confront even today."

Especially today, Kate thought. *Look at Rory and I, wanting to become Ph.D.s in an academic world dominated by so-called scientific thought where only objective proof is validated. If Vine Deloria Jr.'s writing is correct, much of Anthropological evidence isn't evidence at all. Many of the tools they pass off as totally accurate like Carbon Dating, are not exact at all but passed off as perfect by peer validation, even though much of that is really only consensus and group pressure. As Deloria hypothesized, a few Clovis arrow tips dug up, a hypothesized Bering Land Bridge and Anthropologists decreeing that Paleo-Indians followed and wiped out the Mammoths from North America.*

Kate found her voice rising ominously as she continued to lecture her boss. "Look Mr. McBay. After the British North America Act of 1867 John A MacDonald was committed to putting a railroad across the Plains. In order to do that both the buffalo herds had to be eradicated and the First Nations in the Plains, still fierce warriors and capable of violent resistance, had to be subjugated. All that mattered to the new government was grabbing the land, securing the resources and placing settlers on the fertile or semi-fertile areas. After Treaty 6 was negotiated, the promises in that treaty of help during famine and epidemics and farm equipment in Treaty 7 were never kept. Events happened in quick succession.

The buffalo were eradicated leaving Plains Indians without food, shelter, clothes, or a means to obtain any of those things. Whatever farming the Indians had started was destroyed by the Krakatoa Volcano erupting and causing cold weather for two years. Outright starvation resulted and Indians on the Plains, with now weakened immune systems, became even more susceptible to Smallpox, and particularly the Tuberculosis brought by eating the diseased food rations that the government finally supplied. To paraphrase, what happened was close to what the historian James Daschuk calls "ethnic cleansing of the Plains." One third of all the Plains Indians, men, women and children, perished horribly in five years. Neither the Conservative government officials, the Liberals who replaced them or the settlers that now occupied the fertile parts of the land cared. They even welcomed the events. More Indian reserve land was freed for settler occupation.

David Laird and his cronies enforced the Indian Act. Our people were forcibly moved to reserves, unable to hunt and gather, as they had been promised, with the enforcement of the Pass System. They had to obtain passes from Indian agents to even leave the reserve. This left them at the mercy of the government for what were totally inadequate, often rancid and diseased food rations. Our rifles and horses were confiscated. Our children were taken long distances into Industrial Schools in order to break our normal circles of enculturation. Close to fifty percent of children sent into those schools died without adequate food or medical attention. Others were sexually molested.

All this talk of 'Truth and Reconciliation". How can you have either if neither side fully comprehends the value systems that the other believed in and to some extent still believe?"

Kate finally stopped talking as George McBay was staring intensely at her.

"Call me George. Do you realize how attractive you are Kate, that's your name, right, when you get that angry expression on your face? You don't mind if I call you Katie do you?"

Kate felt herself consumed with rage. The one thing she hated more than anything else was being called Katie in a condescending fashion.

"Look Katie, I'm going to consider turning you into a star for this documentary and maybe even for the series if we can get financing. This may be the start of a documentary career, maybe even a movie career for you."

Kate groaned inwardly. Some part of her mind was telling her that a wealthy, super- attractive guy was making her an offer she probably should not refuse but another part was warning her that nothing of any lasting value would come of continued association with her boss. Kate ignored the facial expressions and eye contact signals Rory Broken Head was making for her to tone down her comments. She noticed that he was even shrugging with arm movements that were likely telling her to stop sabotaging the fantastic opportunity they were both being given.

"Look, we need to identify the heroes of Canadian history from both sides of the fence," Kate found herself becoming even more assertive. She wondered why Rory was not saying anything about the heartbreak that Plains Indians had suffered. Pictures of Cree mothers in front of their tattered tipis, without proper clothing, naked from the waist up, without moccasins, kneeling in the snow with their impoverished children, their bones prominent from starvation came into Kate's mind.

Some part of my mind is right, Kate found herself deciding. *Rory only thinks, he doesn't feel.*

"You mean, heroes like my distant cousin David Laird. And Samuel De Champlain and John A. MacDonald. And Alexander Duncan McRae, the man who with his partner, an American banker, flipped most of the land along the C.P.R. railroad to make an immense personal fortune that he turned into a real estate, logging, mining and salmon cannery fortunes in British Columbia in the early twentieth century?"

"Mr. McBay, Alexander Duncan McRae was a robber baron and that was Indian land he and his partners sold to many wealthy American farmers from Minnesota who quickly realized the prairie land could be turned into huge wheat farms. They realized they could sell their farms in Minnesota and make a fortune in the new places."

"Don't say that to my father. Alexander Duncan McRae is one of his heroes. That's why he's financing this film. He wants me to focus on all his Canadian heroes."

What about the Indian heroes? People like Chiefs Tecumseh, Joseph Brant, Pontiac, Poundmaker, Big Bear, Crowfoot and my ancestor, Chief Keenoshayoo. Not to mention female First Nations' heroines like Molly Brant and Pauline Johnson."

"Pauline who?"

Kate groaned inwardly again.

"Pauline Johnson, the great Indian poetess and orator. From the early nineteen hundreds. You know, "The Song My Paddle Sings.""

"A nineteen hundreds, Indian, female, poet? Isn't that an oxymoron? Weren't Indian women called Squaws back then? Whatever did they have to do with poetry? I thought the leading poet at that time was Duncan Campbell Scott."

Kate considered walking out the door without even saying goodbye. She felt herself absolutely consumed with rage.

"Oh my God! You've never heard of Pauline Johnson."

"Relax Katie, you don't mind if I call you that do you?

Kate somehow managed not to scream.

"Of course I've heard of Pauline Johnson. I just think Duncan Campbell Scott was the more important figure for Canadian history. After all, my father says that his policy of Assimilation through the Residential Schools and his unrelenting attack on Indian spirituality was the only real hope for Natives like you to become full citizens of Canada and still is."

Calm down, Katy felt some part of her mind commanded. *Without you this documentary will become a tribute to David Laird, the very man that helped sell out the "Moose Mountain Indian Reservation" from under the feet of your distant relatives. And/or a tribute to Duncan Campbell Scott, the infamous Department of Indian Affairs official who was determined to take the Indian out of the Indian any old way he could manage.*

His policies of Assimilation and Enfranchisement, not to mention criminalizing financing of lawyers for any Indian land claims effectively stopped treaty making from 1923 to 1975. He even managed to have the Potlatch and Sun Dances banned. When Dr. Bryce, the government medical officer pointed out that fifty percent of children attending Residential Schools were dying due to inadequate diet and inadequate care of food preparation he had the position of Medical Officer removed rather than attempt to fix the problems.

Kate could feel pure fury raging through her mind. She could also feel her Sciatica Nerve throbbing extremely painfully.

"Do you know one of the main points Pauline Johnson made in her poetry and prose," Kate protested. "That racism created stereotypes of promiscuous Indian women that cause white men to think them inferior to white women in white men's eyes. Those beliefs set young Indian women up to be sexually hit on and even murdered in extreme cases. The trail of murdered Aboriginal women across Canada since that time and the failure to quickly investigate them still today points to the longevity of such ingrained attitudes."

'Look Katie. I apologize for teasing you. I was just trying to see how photogenic you would become if I got you really angry. I'll have to do that when we are filming. You become extremely photogenic. And I've just had a brainwave. I'll make you the narrator of the documentary. Dressed as Pauline Johnson."

He's just been teasing me, Kate thought. *Don't believe him,* some part of Kate's mind warned her. *He swallowed all the lies his father told him about Indians.*

"Rory what do you think? Do you see what I see? Katie is incredibly beautiful and photogenic when she gets angry. Visualize buckskins on Katie as she reads Pauline Johnson poems. Maybe even having her narrate the entire series I may have to wave a red flag at her or hurl insults at Indians just to get her emotionally charged but we would have the potential for an award-winning documentary."

Kate glared at Rory. She was having a hard time figuring out why Rory was not challenging George McBay's version of Canadian history.

"Uh," Kate could not believe Rory's answer. "You're right Mr. McBay, Kate is very beautiful and photogenic when she's angry. She would make a wonderful Pauline Johnson."

Kate tried to force herself to get control of her surging emotions and flaring back pain but instead found herself losing it completely.

"Pauline Johnson made the point in her poetry and prose that Native women back then were considered inferior to white women. They were seen only setting up and taking down tipis. While they managed every aspect of Indian life for eons, the children, the camp, the cooking, supporting their warrior, or for that matter their fur-trader husband in every way, they were regarded in extremely derogatory fashion by the whites.

Even the Metis of both sexes often had their hearts broken as marriage engagements were broken off with relatives refusing to accept mixed marriages. That's likely what even happened to Pauline Johnson. Her engagement to a prominent white person was broken off suddenly likely because of horrified relatives of the future groom."

"Of course! During the fur trading era and during the early settler years you could simply purchase a fourteen year old Indian maiden for a few dollars and a horse. My father would say that whatever did they know of civilized ways at that time? Indian women were nothing more than concubines."

Kate felt like she was going to have a heart attack. Pure rage was surging through her body. She could feel herself almost disassociating.

"That was after the dominance of the fur traders and after Treaty 6, likely caused by starving families probably thinking that their young daughters would at least get some food. Originally, who do you think managed the enculturation of

the First Nations' Children? It was the Indian mother who taught them all about spirituality and co-existing with all of nature. Unfortunately with the coming of the fur traders and their use of alcohol and guns for trade, many young Indian women were turned into something close to concubines.

Now with the coming of so-called white civilization and the residential schools the children were forced to attend the mothers even had to deal with their offspring being forcibly re-moved and indoctrinated by what Vine Deloria Jr. would call religious fanatics. Half those children never even came home. No wonder the transmission of our culture and spirituality were severely impeded." Kate suddenly stopped as it finally filtered through that it looked like both George McBay and Rory were laughing at her emotional outburst rather than attending to what she was saying.

"Look Katie, I can see that you become more photogenic and articulate the angrier you get. I can see that if we can use you as a narrator we would have a great chance of making an award winning series."

Kate found herself going into some kind of shell-shock. *He's not really processing what you are saying,* some part of her mind warned. *He just sees the potential for star-power you really do possess.*

"Look, you and Rory are going to meet my father tonight. I'll make a bargain with you. I promise we will put some of Pauline Johnson's themes into our documentary if you'll agree to narrate the series. Just don't let my father know. He's a great friend of the anti-Native Casino gambling advocates in the States. You know he's doing everything possible with high placed people to stop Indian casinos. You both have to help me persuade my father to finance more of these documentaries."

"Oh My God! Kate found herself losing it completely de-spite the fact that Rory was waving his arms openly now and put-ting his finger to his lips to silence her. "Your father is against some of the good things the monies from the Native American casinos are doing. Like purchasing lands for their overcrowded reserves. So that some of us can continue to practice our spirituality and belief systems and avoid so-called Assimilation into a consumer-mad society. And you expect me to help convince him he needs to finance more documentaries of the WASP point of view of Canadian history."

"No, you are just going to be the gorgeous face and body that makes the documentary a big hit. I'll tell my father that we are going to feature you as Pauline Johnson. He always talks about how she was a great supporter of Great Britain in her touring shows. For God's sake just smile when he suggests that natives just need to dissolve their reserves and turn everything into fee simple real estate. He really believes that."

Katy's mind went into convulsions as George McBay continued.

"Rory's given me a great idea, Katie. To make a series not just one film. And I've had the brainwave to make you into the narrator of it. I'll try and get my father to increase funding to do a whole series. Meanwhile we'll finish this one about Treaties 5, 6, 7 and 8 and my distant cousin, the Honorable David Laird. Just keep looking beautiful for my father tonight and I promise you that we'll insert some of the other side of the story into the documentaries. We just won't tell my father."

Katy groaned. She made a supreme effort to try and calm down. She mused about the implications of making even more films than she had been contracted for. *I'll never get back to finish my degree,* she sighed. *And George's father is going to insist on featuring David Laird as a hero, I can sense it. He is no hero to modern day First Nations. He negotiated Treaties seven and to eight in his various capacities as first, Lt. Governor of the Northwest Territories, then*

Governor of them and then Indian Commissioner after the treaties took effect. Under him and his orders from the Federal Government he never even honored the terms of the treaties he had negotiated.

My distant relatives, the once tall, healthy, Plains warriors that had successfully hunted the mighty buffalo before guns and horses, were subjugated by disease and starvation before Treaty 8 was negotiated. I'd better try and make George McBay, at least, see the truth about his relative or insert it into the documentary somehow. Kate's emotions and back pain continued to trigger. She found herself lecturing George McBay again.

"You know, your distant cousin was a perfect example of the problems for the Indians that were caused by the Ethno-Centric, world views of the powerful Colonial invaders all over the world."

"Whatever do you mean? My father would say that my cousin's treaties he negotiated guaranteed that a huge area of Canada, the vast area known as Rupert's Land, would become productive rather than sitting idle to no more than nomadic hunters and buffalo herds. He would say that the nomadic hunters did no more than kill the buffalo and waste the rest of the year feasting, gift-giving their wealth away and dancing those primitive dances of theirs to supernatural powers."

Kate found herself choking with rage again.

"The buffalo had been almost completely exterminated by the time your distant cousin negotiated Treaty 8 and my people had been subjugated by epidemics and starvation that the government officials did nothing about despite their promises of a medical chest and help in a famine in Treaty 6. And look at the words you say your father is using, {idle, no more than nomadic hunters of buffalo herds, waste the rest of the year, feasting, gift-giving their wealth away, primitive dances to supernatural powers.}

"So?"

Kate felt herself shaking with rage.

"The Potlatches of British Columbia, the Thirst Dance of the Plains Indians and the Sun Dance were dances of gratitude to the Great spirit that provided all the needs of my people from time immemorial. We didn't hoard resources and build up unbelievable private fortunes by oppressing and marginalizing the rightful owners of the lands. The Sun Dance was dedicated to the bravest of all our warriors who built courage, endurance and overcoming of ego by physical and mental endurance during the Sun dance, qualities that allowed us the ability to hunt the huge, fierce bison, originally with stone-age tools and without horses."

"So why is that relevant to this documentary?"

"Your distant cousin, David Laird, in 1909 in his capacity of Indian Commissioner, banned the Thirst Dance on the reserves that he controlled, reduced the rations of an already impoverished and emaciated people suffering from the bovine Tuberculosis that had been brought in with imported cattle for the new ranchers and the eating of half-rotten beef rations and rancid bacon finally provided by the government. He also had the large Dance Hall that had been built on the Cottonwood Reserve demolished. All to teach what he regarded as people without civilization that they had to become like the Euro-Centric people that had taken over their hunting and gathering lands so that many of the would-be elite, now in government positions, could become fantastically wealthy through corruption and graft."

"Whatever are you talking about?"

"Nepotism, Gerrymandering, political appointments, awarding of lucrative timber and reserve food contracts through fraud and manipulation, cheating Indians by relocating them, then selling their reserve lands, ignoring the Metis's legitimate ownership to the land and buildings they had so long labored to establish, standard Euro-Centric ways of becoming fantastically wealthy."

"Nonsense. Can you prove anything that you are saying?"

"The stories are all here in the history texts. With titles like: [Clearing The Plains: Disease, Politics of Starvation and the Loss of Aboriginal Life], and [The Dispossessed: Life and Death in Native Canada]. Why don't you read some of them?"

"That's what you and Rory are going to be paid for! I just like to get you angry. And I just want you to be a beautiful face, not to mention a vociferous body for the film."

Kate flinched. She was beginning to sense the enormous difficulty of getting anything through to George McBay's head that he did not want to take seriously.

He's really emotionally unavailable, some part of Kate's mind told her. *He lives in sensation, seeks power over others and self-gratification. He's competing with his father in some way. Just go along with him for the time being. Without you this documentary will become like all the other white propaganda about what happened to this country. You know like "The Maple Leaf Forever."*

Oh My God, Kate shuddered. The strains of the Maple Leaf Forever came back to her. "In Days Of Yore Our Hero Wolfe Planted Firm Britannia's Cross On This Our Fair Domain." *Actually it was the Indian's Fair Domain. And the worst part is that I can feel myself somehow attracted to this man. He's sexy, dominant and good looking.*

There you go, some part of Kate's mind chimed in. *Looks again, and you're even attracted to someone who is likely emotionally unavailable if not actually pathologically damaged. And taking time out of your studies. I'm sure you're supposed to be devoting myself to helping your people.*

You will be helping your people, another part of Kate's mind argued. *Make sure this documentary or this series, if George McBay gets more funding, tells it like it was, people of a profit-hungry culture after the land and resources it needed to expand, using methods of expediency if not downright theft for hundreds of years.*

Go with George McBay tonight. Just observe how his father thinks. Many of our people believe somehow that there is still something good in the white, now unbridled, capitalistic system, something that will make members of their governments acknowledge the injustice that our people have suffered for eons and make recompenses for it but they are mistaken. See for yourself. See how they really think. It's only through long, hard and expensive legal action that First Nations people have gained anything at all.

"What is our next location for shooting Katie? George McBay's question jolted Kate out of her musing.

"Around Red River and further North on the river and lake systems, where both my people and the Metis became accidental Canadians in 1867."

"Accidental Canadians, whatever do you mean?"

"Three powerful countries with Imperialistic dreams were competing for the wilds of what would become the Dominion of Canada up to 1867, Britain, the United States and Russia. Before that time the Spanish had decimated the Indians of South America, the Dutch had commoditized what would become New York, and the Portuguese had all but had pulled out completely. If my ancestors had been born in Alaska they would have become accidentally Russian up until Alaska native's land was sold to the United States, oddly enough also in 1867, in which case they became accidental Americans. If my ancestors had been born on the Aleutian Islands under Russian colonization they would have been subjected to incidents involving extreme carnage. For example in the Aleutians, what are now Alaskan islands, natives were lined up in a row and a pistol fired into the chest of the first one just to see how far the shot would go."

"I don't believe that happened."

Kate shook her head. She tried to ignore the fact that some part of her was somehow attracted to another white person in the first place and one that likely had absorbed his father's Racist or at the best, Euro-Centric, extremely negative stereotypes towards First Nations' people as he was growing up.

Kate tried again to get some of the real facts of treatment of Indigenous Peoples in Canada since contact through to George McBay.

"Because the King of England, Charles II by claim of "Divine Right" gave his cousin and main backer of the Hudson's Bay Co., Prince Rupert, title to a huge area of Northern North America called "Rupert's land", and subsequently the Hudson's Bay Co. maintained the British domination of those lands by erecting forts on strategic fur trading routes, my ancestors, the Woods and Plains Cree became accidental Canadians. They became Canadians when the politicians of the new Dominion of Canada decided that the Red River Settlement, occupied mainly by Metis people, who had been the mainstays of and retired from the Hudson's Bay Company with their country wives, and lands north, south, east and west of it, already occupied by First Nations people, were to be part of their domain in 1867. Also to be in the domain were the lands owned by the natives of British Columbia, most of whom had never even made the mark of their totems on treaties as very few were negotiated in that province."

"Nonsense! My father would say that that was all part of the Divine creation of a Great Canadian Nation."

Kate ignored George McBay and went on with her explanation.

"Actually, the natives of British Columbia could well had become accidental Russians had Russia not been intimidated by George Simpson, the Governor of the Hudson's Bay Company, and abandoned their attempts to extend their influence south of the Alaska Panhandle and the fur trade as far south as the Oregon Territory."

"My father would say that you are distorting history but come with me tonight with Rory and I promise that I'll make sure some of your ideas get into this documentary, and series if we get funding, at least some of Pauline Johnson's."

"I'm not distorting history. Actually the natives of what are now the states of Wisconsin, Mississippi, Ohio, Washington and Oregon became accidental Americans when the makers of the Treaty of Ghent that ended the War of 1812 drew a line along the forty-ninth parallel that at least temporarily marked the Canadian/American border. The Iroquois Confederation and other tribes below the forty-ninth parallel in the East, despite the fact that they had fought for the British and assured their victory, were sold out and turned over to the Americans who had a particularly nasty way of dealing with Indians. But now they were accidental Americans. Many of them fled to Canada where they and their descendants became accidental Canadians."

"Will you stop this accidental Canadian business! The Toronto Film Festival isn't going to accept a documentary about that, I can assure you. Do you know where we are filming next Katie?"

"We're headed for Lesser Slave Lake. Along as close as we can get to the original water routes taken by fur traders and treaty makers including your ancestor David Laird and his other treaty makers as they went after the northern lands above the plains where it was already known that there were valuable minerals and petroleum."

"That's right. We are going to film the endeavors of the Honorable David Laird to continue the creation of what would become a wealthy and noble Nation State. We have to put the spotlight on him for my father. Don't ever forget that or we won't have enough money to even complete the first documentary."

"If you say so." Kate was experiencing serious forebodings about trying to function, let alone remain under the control of a boss, who, although, physically very attractive, seemed to have adopted much of his mindset relatively unchanged from the late seventeen hundreds if not before that.

Keep calm, some part of Kate's mind ordered her as she tried to choke back the words that she wanted to say, that she was leaving the employment of George McBay immediately and returning to her studies. *You have to remain grounded, you have to make this documentary more balanced. Pretend to play along. Make him honor his promise to include Pauline Johnson's themes, for example.* Kate winced as a strange mix of hormones and emotions surged through her body. Some part of her was attracted to her boss even though his mindset thoroughly turned her off. *He is so sensuous, so handsome, so assertive, he's a lot like Colin, the white, College boy you had that brief but intense relationship with until he dumped you without explanation.*

"I do say so! Look Katie. Tonight you and Rory and I are having dinner with my father. I'm sorry if I'm going to upset you further but I don't think I can risk introducing you to my father as a First Nation's person at this time. Maybe I can just pass you off as Hawaiian instead of First Nations. You have similar looks to beautiful, Hawaiian women. I've studied them up close when I've vacationed to Oahu."

I bet you have, Kate thought, remembering Rory's warning.

My father will believe you are Hawaiian if I tell him you are. That way when you first meet him you won't be able to talk about the First Nations view of Canadian history and sink this documentary. It's evident that that you get choked up over that view and start to give lectures. Let Rory do the talking. Just sit quietly and be the beautiful face and body that you are."

Kate gasped. "Hawaiian, you want me to pretend to be Hawaiian. You are out of your mind!"

"My father will think you are very beautiful Hawaiian actress," Kate gasped in total disbelief as George McBay ignored her outburst. "Look, I've already seen pictures of the ritual followed at the treaty-signing spots. Flags brought in with canoes, the use of the North West Mounted Police for show and intimidation, the use of feasts at successful treaty signings, cannons firing, you know, shock and awe. My father will be very impressed. He believes in shock and awe.

Bill Mason, the Director of the documentary is getting set up for the Lesser Slave Lake scenes. If we can wrestle more money from my father, we'll shoot some Pauline Johnson scenes, starring you, and make you the narrator of the series. Pauline Johnson's time on this earth was just after Treaty 8, I believe."

You have to carry on with this, some part of Katy's mind ordered. *You have to learn not to react to provocation and external circumstances. Your amygdala fires and you lose it completely. Go and get the first plane back from Vancouver to Calgary,* another part ordered. *You'll be used like the other First Nations' educated people that have allowed themselves to be co-opted by the Multi-National mineral, oil and mining companies.*

Kate found her rational mind floundering as her Sciatica nerve flared into maximum pain.

Oh, no, I can't even think straight when that happens. Kate found herself beseeching a higher power to interfere with the pain. She sank back onto the chesterfield and placed a designer pillow under her left leg. George McBay's voice droned on for what seemed an eternity but finally the pain subsided.

"OK," Kate nodded despite her misgivings as she realized that some part of her mind and from his tone of voice George McBay had decided for her.

"I'll have some Hawaiian history books sent over right away and some tropical print clothes for you to wear at dinner tonight. Rory will help you bone up on Hawaii."

Kate found herself uncharacteristically silent. It was obvious that her employer was not used to people disagreeing with his opinions or orders.

Good, you're learning not to react to extreme provocation, some part of her mind told her. *Go along with this. You'll be able to influence the documentary. You're going to be a big star,* another part of her mind told her, *and the girlfriend of a handsome, wealthy CEO.*

"You're about my size Rory. Borrow some of my clothes for tonight. In the closet in my bedroom. Something casual but elegant. A Sports Coat and slacks should do it and a Polo shirt."

"I'll pick you two up at six o'clock. Just be here in the apartment. Bye now, I've got some business to attend to."

The apartment door slammed. Kate shook her head in disbelief as Rory laughed at her expression.

"He's giving us both a new persona," Kate grimaced at Rory's words.

"At least you get to remain First Nations and can speak. I'm being completely transformed, re-born and reduced to being a pretty face. How come you didn't intervene and back me up about the history?"

"This isn't the time Kate. You really need to tone down your remarks. Look, let's face the facts for a change. This documentary really doesn't have much chance to break even or win awards. From talking with George McBay and after trying myself to promote a more balanced side to Canadian history I know that his father is only going to present the white side of history despite what he says to get you on board. Look I've been working on some more Quilt Histories. Once we get our Ph.D.'s we'll be able to present the real facts with my Quilt portrayals of World Views influence over time and attack prejudices with your Mosaic Awareness Scale. Just be patient. All we have to do is prolong the shooting of the documentary or series. Kate, can't you see that we need the money?"

"Rory, we can't be part of a documentary or series that is only going to justify the Colonial actions that caused irreparable harm to Indigenous people here and other peoples around the world. Look at Africa for instance. The same assumptions of superiority of the British world view and people caused incredible hardship to people in Kenya. The native tribes became landless while white, British settlers set up Colonial mansions in the segregated White Highlands.

They have not even recovered properly to this day. I was reading the other day that some wealthy American was allowed to purchase a huge area for a game farm and the Kenyan natives were forced to move out of the small farms they cultivated. And Indonesia, the country that was handed New Guinea on a silver platter from the United Nations continues to exterminate the aboriginal people there for mass migration of people from Java."

"You're talking to the converted. Have another coffee and some more fruit. There's lots still there left from the breakfast George McBay had brought in. Look Kate, sometimes you have to do strange things to help your people. And think of how our salaries are being drastically improved. We might both be able to do a Doctorate program. Think Dr. Kate Golden Eagle, Dr. Rory Broken Head. Then we will help our people."

Kate was still trying to compose her thoughts an hour later as Rory kept trying on George McBay's clothes. *My Sciatica Nerve is still acting up. But maybe Rory is right, we have to do strange things to help our people.*

Kate's musing stopped as she looked up and let out a sigh of admiration as Rory stood in front of her looking very handsome in what was certainly a casual but elegant outfit. His muscular build completely filled George McBay's Polo shirt and Sports jacket.

"You look gorgeous. Look out, Mr. McBay is likely to turn you into a Tahitian prince or something like that."

"Why are you still lying on the chesterfield with your left leg under a pillow?"

"The back injury I received playing basketball. The Sciatica Nerve started flaring when George McBay said he had never heard of Pauline Johnson."

"Your back injury must be in your head, Kate. You know Psychosomatic. Maybe it flares when your point of view is not supported."

"Thanks!"

Both of them jumped as the apartment buzzer rang.

"Delivery for Katie Golden Eagle," a voice box buzzed. Minutes later Rory was astounded as he pulled out several books about Hawaii, two elegant Hawaiian print dresses and what were obviously very expensive, dress sandals.

"Our boss doesn't waste time does he? Try this on," Rory ordered. Kate went into the bedroom and obliged.

"Wow, that outfit should do it," Rory exclaimed. "You look awesome. That dress really shows off your figure. Take it off and we'd better read these books. Even though you're supposed to be silent you'll likely have to answer a few questions about Hawaii."

Kate sighed deeply as she reached for a book entitled "Hawaii's Story By Hawaii's Queen."

"Hawaii had a Monarchy," she told Rory in surprise some time later. "Somehow I thought Hawaii was always part of the United States."

Both of them were still reading hours later when the apartment door flew open and George McBay came rushing in. Kate glanced at her watch. He was early. She watched as he glanced at the clothes in one of the armchairs.

"You've got good taste, Rory, that's my favorite Sports Jacket and shirt. Try the clothes on for me, will you. I want to make sure you look all right for this dinner party. My father and several of his business cronies, as well as my brother Arthur and his wife are going to be there."

"Perfect," he announced. Kate gasped as her boss pulled out a jewelry box and opened it. Inside was a very beautiful shell necklace. She felt her face turn red as he placed it around her neck and Rory whistled in approval.

"Those shells are from the Hawaiian Island of Niihau. I picked the necklace out for you myself. The shells are harvested only once a year as they float in from the ocean."

"You look gorgeous Kate," Kate felt her face burning at Rory's compliment.

"So tell me what you know about Hawaii, Kiana?"

"Kiana?"

"That's Hawaiian for Diana. You have become Kiana Kealoha, my new protégée. Rory you are now Rory McTavish, a goods Scots name. I know many of my father's Scottish ancestors took country wives."

"What's wrong with my real name?" Kate was glad to hear Rory finally question something.

"My father is not going to fund a series with Rory Broken Head as the History expert, believe me. Now Katie, tell me a brief history of Hawaii."

You should have taken the first plane back to Calgary, some part of Kate's mind warned her. *You and Rory are being co-opted. This is a great opportunity for you and Rory,* another part advised *and you have to get both sides of the story into this documentary or, God Forbid, even series.* Kate felt completely confused as she obeyed the order to talk about Hawaiian history. She could feel her Sciatica nerve acting up again although she had not done anything physical to injure it.

Maybe Rory's right, my back pain is Psychosomatic?"

"The Hawaiian monarchs converted to Christianity, set up a western system of government, turned their lands into private ownership, formed treaties of Neutrality with most nations at that time including England, France, and the U.S.A. Despite the treaties America, through the American Minister Stevens, helped overthrow the constitutional monarch in 1893. He had

Marines off the USS Boston stand in front of the American coup organizers, mostly the avaricious sons of some the very missionaries who had come in 1820. Had the Queen fired on the Marine she would have been declaring war on the United States. The United States completely seized Hawaiian lands and power in 1898 when it annexed the Islands as a Territory.

I thought Canadian Indians had it bad. The Hawaiians don't even have a treaty of any kind with their colonizer. They don't even have the recognition given to Native Americans or Native Alaskans. Their land has been turned into luxury hotels and gated communities for the rich."

"Not that history! The history after Hawaii became a State in 1959. Emphasize how Hawaii is now a first class tourist destination. These are business people at the dinner not social workers or radical activists."

You should have remained at the documentary shoot, Kate's mind advised again. This time there was no comment from the other part of her mind.

"No glasses either. You look less intellectual but more beautiful without them."

Kate gasped. "But Mr. McBay, I'm very near-sighted. I really can't see well at all without them."

"Call me George, and just manage tonight without your glasses. Don't worry. Rory or me will be at your side and do the seeing for you. Tomorrow we'll have you fitted for contact lenses or maybe even have Laser Surgery done. You'll be even more photogenic."

Oh My God! Kate mused, *Rory is now becoming a seeing-eye dog of Scottish origin. And Laser Surgery. I've heard horror stories from a few people who haven't been able to read afterwards. I might become one of them. I'll never get through my studies even if I ever get back to them.*

Chapter 3. Final Preparations For Funding Requests.

Two hours later after a drive through Vancouver rush-hour traffic into the expensive Point Grey area, Kate found herself completely discombobulated as she sat in between Rory and George McBay staring across the table without her glasses at Chuck McBay, George's father. Kate could not see him clearly but could tell he was a very large man. His voice was even louder than his son's.

"What kind of name is Kiana" demanded the blurry figure "or for that matter, Kealoha?"

"Kiana is Hawaiian for Diana," Kate tried to keep her voice rather quiet, and Kealoha means with love."

"I know what aloha means," the loud voice replied. Others at the table laughed. Kate tried to remember their names but without her glasses could not attach the names to hardly anyone she saw at the table.

"Indeed you do. George and I have had a succession of step mothers to prove that." Kate recognized the voice if not the blurry image of George McBay's younger brother, Arthur. *A gasp from the other side of the table likely emanated from the senior McBay's present wife, Georgina,* Kate mused. *I can't see her clearly but from her voice I bet Georgina isn't much older than her step sons.*

George's brother Arthur was introduced as the CEO of McBay Resources, his father's company. I wonder why the younger brother was chosen to lead the company rather than George, Kate mused. *That's part of the problem,* some part of Kate's mind informed her, *sibling rivalry. George's father has always favored his younger son. George was too impulsive for him. Chuck McBay tried to bring his older son to heel by promoting his younger brother over him but George is still being obstinate.*

"So what make you think that this film venture of yours has more chance of success than all your other failed ventures?" It was Arthur's voice again.

"And you want to drag more money out of me," George McBay's father snorted as if to reinforce the words of his youngest son.

"This lady right here," Kate felt her face turning bright red as her boss 's words made her the center of everybody 's attention. "We'll turn her beauty into our advantage. Make her into Pauline Johnson and have Kiana recite the poems that pay tribute to England and the glory of Britain. Like "Canadian Born.""

"Well Kiana is a beaut all right," Kate felt her face going even redder as she could see blurry figures turning in her direction and felt their concentrated stares. "And I like the idea of promoting our British heritage, particularly our relative that had everything to do with the Treaties that removed those mineral and petroleum rich, huge territories from any vestige of Indian ownership, the Honorable David Laird." Kate found herself pressing her fingernails into the palms of her hands instead of speaking out like she would normally have done.

"I don't think you have enough dramatic history to interest Canadians in a series, TV or otherwise," Arthur challenged.

"That's right Arthur," his father echoed, "what makes you think you can overcome that problem? Everybody believes that Canadian history is boring beyond belief."

"This fellow here is going to solve that problem. My history expert, Rory McTavish. He's an expert at finding material that would make a series irresistible to a Canadian audience. Liven up their history so to speak. Rory tells me there's a lot of gossip-type material in Canadian history. It's just been left out of all the dry accounts."

"Such as? And isn't that fellow wearing your Sports Jacket?" Kate shuddered as Geoge McBay's brother tried to humiliate him.

"We both just have excellent taste. "Rod McBay laughed his brother's comments off but Kate could tell he had issues of longstanding with his brother. She picked up his seething anger. "Give them an example of the gossip, Rory."

Kate gulped but quickly relaxed a bit as Rory told a little known story about Sir William Johnson, the Superintendent of Indian Affairs in the mid seventeen hundreds appointed by the British and given a Baronet. He made a fortune in the Mohawk Valley before and after his success in bringing the Iroquois Confederation to the side of the British cause in the French/Indian wars.

"Sir William was a legendary figure in his time. He was rumored to have fathered over seven hundred Indian children. He was a larger than life character brought to what is now New York from Ireland by his uncle a British Naval Hero. Somehow he learned the Mohawk language, was able to charm the Mohawks and led them in myriads of battles against the French and their supporters in Canada and particularly in the Mohawk Valley."

"Why is that scandalous?" Kate winced as Chuck McBay queried Rory.

"When Molly Brant, the famous Indian heroine of the American Revolution, first met Sir William she leapt up onto his horse behind him, survived his attempt to have his horse throw her off, and enchanted the Baronet as he eventually assisted her in dismounting. They looked into their other's eyes and remained together for the rest of his life. Molly was already a highly connected Indian Princess with diplomatic and strategic skills. She displaced his so called housekeeper, became his country wife and bore him nine children until his death in 1774. Molly Brandt, her brother Joseph and William's son and heir Sir Guy Johnson were the reason most of the Iroquois Confederation remained loyal to Britain during the War of 1812."

"Well, I suppose that does have possibilities," Kate was glad to hear Chuck McBay admit. "What else?'

"Then there is Sir Clifford Sifton, the Interior Minister of the new Alexander MacKenzie government that made a small fortune out of his Cabinet appointment. MacKenzie's Minister of the Interior got caught exiting the back door of a fellow Minister's house," Rory related, "after the fellow came home late in the evening and surprised his wife who pretended she was alone in the house." The dinner table guests laughed uproariously as Rory managed to extract several gossipy type events from his knowledge of Canadian history.

"And once Ottawa had subjugated the Plains Indians and had them under the full control using the Indian Act, actual Indian Affairs officials were caught in a series of scandals that involved sexual predation with very young Indian girls."

Thank God! Kate mused. *Rory's become the source of attention. The heat is off of me, at least for the moment.*

"All right, I'll consider moving your documentary film into a series," Kate was astonished to hear from George McBay's father after several of Rory's tales. Send me several scripts outlining possible scenes and I'll give the matter serious consideration."

"We'll need interim funding in the meantime. That way we can save money by not doubling back on locations."

"I'll advance some interim money but you have a week to get those scenes to me in written form. Before I go to the States. Include a revised business plan. I need to be sure you have a good possibility of making a profit this time."

"You had better get a second opinion," Kate could not believe George McBay's brother's protest.

"Since when have I needed a second opinion," his father sneered.

What a loving family, Kate mused.

Two hours later Kate felt a little better as she was able to put on her glasses again. They were back in her boss's apartment and George McBay was demanding that Rory start working immediately on the scenes that his father had insisted on.

"Well the first scene we should paint is one that shows the Plains Cree and Blackfoot Indians before they were decimated by disease and starvation into subjugation in time for Treaty 8."

"Why?"

"Because the fact that the warriors of the Cree and the Blackfoot were in great shape in 1867 when Sir John A. MacDonald wanted to build a railroad across the plains to the west to cement the new Dominion of Canada from sea to sea necessitated treaties being done in the first place. King George III in 1763 issued orders under his Proclamation that Indian title West of Ontario had to be extinguished by Chiefs signing treaties at a large public meeting they had been invited to for that purpose. Also, Sir John A. wanted to avoid expensive Indian wars like the ones taking place in the U.S. The wars in the U.S. were costing twenty million dollars a year to wage, more than the entire budget of the new Dominion of Canada."

"You know the real reason George III issued that proclamation?"

"No Kate I don't."

"Dutch merchants and other wealthy settlers in the American Colonies were getting Indians drunk, having them put x's on deeds for lands they likely didn't even have the right to sell and buying up Indian lands in the Mohawk Valley and other areas bordering on the colonies as individuals. George III did not want that to happen in what would become Canada. He wanted Indian land only surrendered or sold to the Crown itself. That's really why he insisted that treaties be done for lands west of what would become Thunder Bay. It was not for some kind of humanitarian motive."

"You're absolutely right Kate but we don't need a scene showing that at the moment."

"Right," Kate found Rory's words depressing. "But showing a scene with the healthy, warlike Blackfoot and Cree in the midst of a buffalo hunt would get across the idea of the strength of the Plains warriors at that time. They were formidable. They were the healthiest of all the Eastern and Central First Nations people as the buffalo had provided everything they needed. Dried, pounded pemmican laced with berries was a sound, nutritious diet. Buffalo hides provided coverings for tipis and tanned buffalo hides provided warm clothes and moccasins for the harsh winters. Buffalo skulls were used in spiritual practices. Our culture and people were healthy, war-like, spiritual and strong still on the Plains."

Kate listened as Rory painted in the scene. Fierce buffalo everywhere with Indians in full costume on horseback pursuing the stampeding animals. He told George McBay that he would create an action scene impressing the audience with the power and courage of the First Nations warriors. He went on to relate how he would create a scene with Sir John A. MacDonald and some of his ministers talking about the necessity of making treaties to avoid an all-out expensive Indian war and plotting how to word the treaties to prevent much expense in the future.

The Metis would be left out entirely or offered script for land by separate Half-Breed Commissioners that would accompany the Indian Treaty Commissioners. The Treaty Commissioners knew that script would almost always be selected by the Metis as the difficulty of travelling to land offices to find and register land presented enormous obstacles at that time. The government officials knew that the script would immediately be sold to profiteers thereby ending any future payments. Rory elaborated that he would create a scene where Surveyors and telegraph people were being turned back by warriors as was happening at that time.

He told George McBay that he would create another scene with one of the ministers proposing a semi-military, police force being sent ahead into the area to intimidate the Indians as well as the rowdies and liquor dealers from the states who were already invading the territory. Rory told his boss that Government discussion at that time led to the start of the Northwest Mounted Police.

And then we'll show scenes of the talented Northwest Territories Governor Alexander Morris as he used a number of methods to negotiate Treaties 5, and 6. including adopting the treaty-making protocols of the Hudson Bay Company. He used ritual established by the Hudson's Bay Company way back in time. Hudson's Bay Factors had long adopted the actual kin-ship ceremonies they had been forced to practice to make peace and trade agreements with Indian nations. From way back rituals had been used by Indian nations to adopt warriors they captured in wars. That way they could replace members of their own tribes killed in battle and keep their population numbers up.

To the Indians these ceremonies were sacred, binding agreements. The use of the Peace Pipe signified the presence of the Great Spirit. The same ceremonies were used with the Hudson Bay Officials to solemnize the trading agreements.

The rituals included peace and friendship agreements from the very beginning of the Hudson's Bay Company in Canada. Gift-giving, use of the Pipe, cannon firing, feasting, medals, etc. were used for Treaties 5 and 6 plus the red coats of the North West Mounted Police. This was to allow the Woods and Plains Cree as well as other tribes to think it was the British Queen they were still dealing with instead of the rapacious, land and mineral seekers of the new settler governments of Upper Canada, the Maritimes and Lower Canada who were determined to expand their empires. The Cabinet of the new Dominion government was also trying to prevent the even more rapacious American politicians and capitalists who considered it their "Manifest Destiny" to own all of North America and even all of South America.

"Your father will be pleased," Rory added. Kate flinched as Rory described how Governor Alexander Morris had gained surrender of the fertile belt around both the North Saskatchewan and South Saskatchewan Rivers by use of Hudson Bay Company treaty making ritual, its association with Queen Victoria who was seen as beneficial compared to the Long knives of the U.S. Calvary, and taking advantage of disagreement amongst the Chiefs themselves when some chiefs showed themselves in agreement with treaty making?

Kate flinched further as Rory described how Morris included promises of a medicine chest and help for famine as well as schools in order to persuade the hard bargainers in Treaty 6 to sign.

"That was his mistake," Rory concluded. "Morris was removed by the new Alexander MacKenzie government, a frugal Scots group who resented the extra costs for medicine or food rations for a possible famine or epidemic that Morris had agreed to. That was when David Laird was brought back from Prince Edward Island, a Clear Grit true and true as the Reform Liberals were then called, a man who could be relied on to keep costs down. Your father will be proud.

We'll have a scene of the newly created North West Mounted Police heading out of Toronto to set out to the Plains to eliminate the firewater traders, intimidate the Plains Cree and Blackfoot, and bring law and order not to mention Dominion of Canada control to the fertile lands bordering the North and South Saskatchewan Rivers. The Mounted police will be on their specially selected show horses and be wearing the Red Serge uniforms and white helmets reminiscent of former British regulars. We'll show their ending of Fort Whoop Up, where American traders over the border from Montana traded virulent firewater for buffalo robes with extremely detrimental effects on the Indians.

Kate's Sciatica nerve flared as Rory outlined David Laird's accomplishment of the completion of Treaty 7. The treaty making took place at Blackfoot Crossing and involved surrender of all of Southern Alberta. The Treaty encampment featured a large contingent of North West Mounted Police in their Red Serge dress uniforms. Blackfoot and Cree chiefs still wore their traditional Aboriginal outfits and camped in their traditional tipis somewhat distant from the Treaty Commissioners and the North West Mounted Police. Rory told of David Laird's statement that local laws had been passed to stop Metis from hunting the remainder of the buffalo thereby assuring a food supply for the immediate future. Rory told of promises to supply cattle for raising stock, promises that their mobility and freedom to hunt would not be interfered with and promises of a Winchester rifle, medal and flag for the chiefs right away.

Kate's Sciatica nerve flared even more as she remembered that costly promises from Treaty 6 of a medicine chest, a school on the reserves, and protection from famine were deliberately left out of the agreement in Treaty 7. The Indian Act had already been brought into existence but David Laird made no mention that Indians who thought they were negotiating sacred treaties between equals to share the resources of the land would now become child-like wards in the eyes of the Canadian Government. Kate knew that four years later massive protest would erupt at Blackfoot Crossing at another meeting when Lord Lorne, Queen Victoria's son-in-law and Governor General of Canada, visited during a tour of Canada. At that meeting The Cree and Blackfoot would be protesting aggressively over the breaking of all the promises except the rifle, medal and flag.

"That's great Rory," Kate's thoughts were interrupted as her boss congratulated her friend. "We'll carry on with some more scenes but you had better retire for the night Katie. You are having Laser Surgery on both your eyes tomorrow morning at 9:00 a.m. I'll have a driver take you to the clinic and pick you up later."

"Both eyes! I thought they did only one eye at a time and three months later did the other eye in case something went wrong with the first. And I've heard that sometimes reading function is affected. I'm a graduate student. I can't afford to have my reading eyesight negatively affected."

"You really only need one eye Katie, even if something unforeseen does happen to one of them. But I'll restrict the surgery to one eye, I promise. We'll have to take the chance. We need to shoot some Pauline Johnson scenes as soon as we get back. Don't worry. The Laser surgery is paid for already. We'll do the other eye in three months as you request."

"How is that going to work? I'll be able to see perfectly with one eye and not at all in the other."

"Don't worry about it. I promise it will be all right."

The next afternoon Kate found herself with a covering over one eye being led back to the apartment by a driver. Rory helped her to lie down on a chesterfield.

"I'll do you packing for you Kate. We have to catch a plane back to Saskatchewan in a few hours."

"I can't see. I'm supposed to have the Laser surgery checked in a few days."

"George says he'll have you flown back into Vancouver to do that. In the meantime just wear sun glasses to keep the glare out."

"George?"

"Mr. McBay insists you and I call him George."

"What about our Mosaic questionnaire and our Quilt project?"

"We'll do those for our Ph.D.'s Kate. In the meantime you need to locate some of Pauline Johnson's poetry praising Canada that you can recite for one of the scenes we are going to shoot for George's father. You need to also locate some of her poetry or prose about Indian concerns. We'll insert those in later scenes that George's father is not going to see immediately."

"How am I supposed to locate the poetry?"

George had a complete compilation of Pauline Johnson's work sent over already. It's in that box. Remind me to pick it up on the way out."

"How am I supposed to read that material?"

"I'll help you with it, I promise."

Chapter 4. Frenzied Schedule.

Several days later Kate sat on a director's chair in Regina, Saskatchewan trying to remember by heart several passages of Pauline Johnson's poetry that greatly praised Canada. George McBay had hastily arranged for a film studio to shoot the start of her Pauline Johnson scenes as well as the start of the film's narration. Other revised scenes were being shot in the Southern Alberta area where David Laird had assisted with Treaty six and had been the chief government negotiator for Treaty 7.

Kate was dressed in similar buckskins to the ones that the real Pauline Johnson wore as part of her stage act including a replica of the British Army red colored Broadcloth blanket that her father, Mohawk Chief George Johnson, had given Queen Victoria's son, Prince Albert, Duke of Connaught, and Governor General of the Dominion of Canada, as he was touring Canada. The young Prince had come to Chiefswood, Pauline's family residence on the Grand River near Brantford Ontario, to be initiated into the Iroquois Confederation as a legitimate Chief of the Six Nations when he had visited Canada. He was given the name Karakoulige which meant "the sun flying from East to West under the guidance of the Great Spirit."

Pauline Johnson's father was always extremely loyal to the British Crown, Kate mused. *I guess the Iroquois Confederation Chiefs thought that by becoming one of them the young Prince would be obliged to act on their behalf. How wrong they were.* Kate stared in horror at what she recognized as a scalp dangling from the wampum belt that Pauline Johnson always wore in her recitals.

"I hope this isn't a real scalp," Kate complained to George McBay who was supervising the shoots to be sent to his father himself.

"Of course not. Take off your sunglasses," he ordered as the Director motioned her to move into the spotlight for filming.

"I need the sunglasses. I can't get my eyes to function together. I can only see out of one eye at a time. The left sunglass has a prescription so both eyes can function together. The right one is just glass."

"Never mind! You don't need to see. You're much more photogenic without the glasses."

Kate obeyed but the glare of the camera lights really hurt her eyes. She realized she would have to stop her tendency to close one eye to see clearly. She could feel tears flowing in her eyes.

"That's great," George McBay's words boomed across the set. "You look much more authentic with the tears."

Kate stared blindly into the lights of the camera. She managed to ignore the pain in her right eye so soon after her recent Laser Eye surgery. She pulled the words of Pauline's poem "Canadian Born," out of her memory.

"We first saw light in Canada, the land beloved of God: We are the pulse of Canada, its marrow and its blood:

And we, the men of Canada, can face the world and brag

That we were born in Canada beneath the British flag.

Few of us have the blood of kings, few are of courtly birth,

But few are vagabonds or rogues of doubtful name and worth;

And all have one credential that entitles us to brag—

That we were born in Canada beneath the British flag."

"That's super," Kate was amazed at being praised by her boss as she finished the rest of the patriotic poem and was allowed to return to her seat. "Your tears really emphasize how Pauline loved Canada. My father will be very pleased."

"Oh My God," Pauline confessed her agony to Rory later when the shoot had finished for the day and they were back in her trailer. "Our Ancestors were born in Indian Country and were humiliated, starved, called wards or children of the Queen, marginalized and oppressed by Ministers of the Government of Canada. Rupert's Land was transferred to the Dominion of Canada with the Hudson's Bay Company being given three hundred thousand pounds and twenty percent of the fertile land instead of the legitimate owners, the Plains and Northern Indians and the Inuit.

Several of our chiefs were publicly hanged after the Riel Rebellion, our innocent leaders were jailed, and our horses and guns confiscated. We got the meagre sum of five to twelve dollars a year, the Indian Act, which confined us to reserves located on second-rate land at the government's mercy, and our chiefs got a rifle, a flag and a medal."

"Don't worry Kate. You won't be blamed for this documentary. No one from our world will recognize you anyway. You're without glasses, being introduced as Kiana Kealoha, and likely that scene will only be seen by George's father with any luck."

Rory's words did nothing to appease Kate's fears. Her Sciatica Nerve flared painfully.

You'll have to move out of the Prairies when this film surfaces, one part of her mind told her. You and Rory will become Ph.D.'s another part argued, you can do a lot for your people then.

"Brace yourself, after this we are going to start shooting the scenes where David Laird and his fellow commissioners brave the waters of the Saskatchewan and Athabasca Rivers to reach Lesser Slave Lake to meet the Chiefs that are to sign Treaty 8. I have to go and help paint the scenes for George right now."

"We are being co-opted Rory."

"We need the money for Ph.D.'s. My brother killed himself because he couldn't get the funding to proceed past his Masters. I'm doing this for him. With any luck no one will ever see this film anyway, it's so unbalanced."

That's why Rory is humiliating himself by working on this documentary. He's doing it for his brother. That explains it.

But why are you doing this? Some part of Kate's mind questioned her. *My Sciatica Nerve is acting up again,* she mused. Kate collapsed on the uncomfortable bed of the small travel trailer on the film studio lot she had been assigned in despair.

Treaty 8, that's where a few First Nations signed treaty at Lesser Slave Lake and then near Fort St. John, B.C. A huge territory comprising most of Rupert's Land was considered surrendered by that Treaty and most of the chief's within it were not even contacted, the commissioners started so late in the season, Kate mused as she sank into an exhausted sleep.

Several days later Kate was on the shore of the Athabasca River. She clutched the sheets of the narration she was told to do as camera men filmed the actors portraying David Laird and the other commissioners of Treaty 8 sitting on scows being pulled from shore by gangs of Metis and First Nations men. The men were attached by ropes as they dragged the scows up the shores of the mighty Athabasca River towards Lesser Slave Lake. The actors portraying Metis were having a hard time of it along with actors portraying North West Mounted Police who had volunteered to help with the tracking of the boats in 1898 when the crew originally contracted did not show up.

Kate found herself in some kind of mind induced trance. Treaty 8 was negotiated *thirteen long years after Treaty 7,* she mused. *David Laird was told to quickly get First Nations people to surrender the Central and Northern portions comprising Rupert's Land when both oil and gold were discovered in northern reaches of the huge area. Her readings of history revealed that since Treaty 7 government policy meant that only when resources were found or settlers approaching were any more treaties to be done despite the worsening conditions for both the Plains and Woods Indians. However in 1890 petroleum discoveries were made in the Athabasca and MacKenzie River districts. Railroads were needed to move minerals and salt, the bi-products of* petroleum production, and gold had been discovered in the Klondike of B.C.

Kate choked on the words that she was forced to narrate portraying David Laird and his fellow commissioners as heroes.

She turned to George McBay who was seated next to her and told him how by 1879 the buffalo herds were no more and their Plains people had no housing, no clothes, no food and no medicine or doctors as famine, Tuberculosis and Smallpox ravaged their tribes. The promises of agricultural assistance had not been kept. She relayed how The 1876 Indian Act turned Indians into legal children and they became administered people. Promises to allow bands to select their own reserves were not kept. They were moved from the fertile Cypress Hills in S.W. Saskatchewan and S. W. Alberta. Kate related how the government had even closed Fort Walsh in the Cypress Hills to cut off even the inadequate food rations and force movement to the Qu'Appelle Valley so the land could be given to incoming settlers.

She related to George McBay how in the 1880's Indians were forced to work to receive any food, stopping them from any hunting activity only to receive often rancid bacon in return. In 1883 the government cut allocations for food relief and agricultural assistance. They had decided to civilize the Indians and set up so-called Industrial schools to force bands to send children to distant residential schools.

"Despite all that my people did not become violent, they tried petitions and protests when Lord Lorne toured the prairies in 1881."

"What about the Riel Rebellion?"

"That was a Metis rebellion. It happened after the Metis were not assured to title of their holdings in the Red River Valley. Many of the Metis who had worked for the Hudson's Bay Company had built homes for their families there and found they did not possess proper title to the land. Suddenly the newly created Government of the Dominion of Canada was telling them that surveyors would decide what lands they would have and that the surveys would involve square plots not the long plots they already had that gave them river access.

They rebelled thinking that the now starving Cree and Blackfoot Indians would join their newly created Provisional Government. However only a small number of the Indians joined them. The other Indians honored the promises they had given in Treaties five and six to remain faithful to the Crown. The Metis were defeated when thousands of Dominion soldiers were moved close enough by the new CPR railroad to march to Batouche where the Metis were pinned down and staging a shootout with other government soldiers.

The defeat and the hanging of Riel plus several Indians who had taken part in the rebellion followed. The Riel Rebellion was used by the government as an excuse to further subjugate and humiliate our chiefs. Our leadership was eliminated. Influential chiefs like Poundmaker and Big Bear were placed into prison, contracted Tuberculosis there and died soon afterwards when they were released. Cree and Blackfoot horses and guns were confiscated.

The government now had a railroad system to bring thousands of troops from Toronto, a telegraph system to alert them of any Indian meetings and the implementation of a draconian "Pass System" where in order to even leave a reserve for the day or otherwise our people had to have permission from an Indian agent. That was hardly in keeping with the promises of Treaties 3 to7 of mobility for hunting and gathering."

"We'll discuss this in more detail once we shoot the Lesser Slave Lake shots, Katie. I want you and Rory to come back with me to Vancouver so you can support me when I show these scenes to my father."

Kate quelled her misgivings and moved into the spotlight as she narrated the scenes Rory had written. She forced herself to speak of the hardships the commissioners had endured as their scows and barges were towed by Metis trackers up the sand bars and windfalls along the river. She spoke of them enduring endless rain and thunderstorms while in actual fact they were seated comfortably on the York boats and stayed in their tents while their work force of Indians and Metis took care of the cooking and physical tasks involved.

What struck Kate forcibly was the contrast between the scenes in Treaty 7, when the Blackfeet and Cree were still healthy and dressed in their traditional clothes and the scenes in Treaty 8 where the more northern First Nations people had already adopted western clothing, haircuts and appearances. Photos of her distant relative, Chief Keenoshayoo, revealed him wearing a western style jacket, pants and even shoes in place of moccasins.

No wonder, some part of Kate's mind told her, *they had no choice. Trappers coming from the States had already strip-mined their fur areas, wiping out all the fur-bearing animals in them and then moving onto another area unlike the natives themselves, who were always content to leave enough of the animals to allow breeding to continue. Winters had also been extremely harsh in 1883 and 1884 eliminating even more of the game animals.*

You know the Hudson's Bay Company had already denied credit to the natives once other traders were allowed to enter the vast areas of the North and compete with the Hudson's Bay people. Once that happened there was no way for the natives to get provisions to make it through to the next fur trapping harvest.

How sad, Kate mused. *My people were forced to sign treaties just to get the meagre annuities that they thought would help them survive those terrible times.*

And the injustice of the script system. Metis could get government script for land from the Half-breed Script Commissioners that came along with David Laird and his Treaty 8. The government knew that the Metis would mainly sell their script that guaranteed land to the hordes of speculators following the commissioner. Otherwise they would have to travel huge distances to the registry office to locate and register any land they may have wanted. The script went for a few cents on the dollar. It was a great way to remove any future land base from the Metis.

What a circus, Kate mused as she viewed the recreation of the Lesser Slave Lake Treaty Site. Around the Treaty Commission Marquee and the other tents holding the food for the feast after the treaty signing were an array of debauchery sites, tents for eating, tents for dancing, tents for gambling away script or the money received for it and of course, tents for buying liquor.

That was so many of the Metis receiving script and even some of the natives choosing script for land would be tempted to sell it for a few cents on the dollar. The Metis were given only the script to silence any resistance rather than annuities. That way the new Government of Canada would have no financial obligation to the Metis once their script had been disposed of.

Then it got worse. Helicopters flew Kate and the actor portraying David Laird up to Lake Athabasca where Kate had to witness the signing of several more band chiefs who were forced to surrender their people's land for the same terms that the Lesser Slave Lake tribes had been given. Kate realized as she flew over huge areas of land that David Laird and even his two other Treaty Commissioners who had moved towards the Yukon territory met with only a few of the tribes occupying Rupert's Land. She wondered how the Government of Canada had presumed they had legally carried out their obligation under the Proclamation of 1763 to extinguish native title without even contacting most of the tribes in the huge area or holding the public meeting required.

"We've got enough scenes filmed to show my father," George McBay stated a month and a half later as he suddenly reappeared on the scene again. "I want you and Rory to come back and be with me as father watches these scenes. We have to do everything possible to convince him to provide the extra funding for a full series. I am running out of funds."

Chapter 5. Happy Family.

Days later Kate sighed as she found herself alone with George McBay in his luxurious apartment overlooking the ocean from Vancouver's West End.

"Where's Rory?"

"He'll be here tomorrow. He had to help edit some of the scenes we just shot."

Oh my God! Kate suddenly realized she was alone with the Producer in his apartment. *But George McBay has never done anything or said anything that was out of place before, he's had other chances, it must be all right.*

Kate decided she had a chance to push for some scenes that would give a fairer version of what really happened on the Prairies and Northern Canada in the late 1880's and 1890's.

"You know that in her prose Pauline Johnson has some very detrimental things to say about the Qu'Appelle Industrial School. She toured it in the early 1900's and reported that the students were very docile and depressed. Several of her poems directly accuse the invading hordes of Euro-Centric immigrants and their government of taking the land, attacking native spiritual beliefs and having the nerve to send missionaries here when the slums and injustices in England itself were rampant."

"This is a good time to discuss what you think we should add to the series, Katie. I've got some dinner and entertainment planned for us. They're filming a new series for The Aboriginal People's Television Network in Vancouver. A series featuring

Aboriginal musicians in collaboration. I've managed to get tickets."

"Really! I've heard about that series. Thanks, I'd love to see one of its programs being filmed."

"Put on one of those tropical print dresses. I've brought you some more clothes for when we'll have to do publicity on the documentary. There's a jacket you will look lovely in back in the second bedroom. I'll change into a suit and we'll go out for dinner first."

Kate was astonished at George McBay's apparent change in attitude. *He's willing to talk about my input into future scenes,* she mused. Kate gasped as she opened the closet in the back bedroom. A virtual wardrobe was present. Dresses, suits, slacks, shoes, blouses, sweaters and jackets. All in her size. She could see immediately the jacket he wanted her to wear tonight. She quickly picked out the dress that George had liked at his father's dinner party and added the new jacket and some dress shoes.

He even knows my shoe size, she mused in astonishment.

"You look gorgeous, Beautiful," Kate found herself feeling considerable warmth around her heart at his words and his intense glance of approval.

"And don't let anyone tell you that you have no future in narrating documentaries or for that matter acting in them. You are doing a first rate job on this film."

Watch out, some part of Kate's mind warned her. *He's very attracted to you.*

What's wrong with that? Kate realized she was irritated at the warning. *Maybe I can influence some of these scenes for the better,* she retaliated. *I'm finally receiving validation of my work from an influential white person. Maybe Rory is wrong. Maybe this documentary will become more balanced and be seen by myriads of people.*

An hour later Kate found herself sitting beside George McBay at a smorgasbord featuring Prime Rib. The expensive restaurant featured a small dance floor with a place for musicians at the back of the dining area.

"Red wine or white?"

"Red, thanks." Kate was impressed as her boss gave the waiter orders for a brand of wine she had never heard of.

He's so sophisticated, she thought. *And I'm just a backwater person.*

"A Shooting Sherry," he explained. "It goes well with the Prime Rib."

An hour later Kate found herself quite relaxed as she and her boss consumed the bottle of Sherry. They worked their way through a meal of Prime Rib, salad, and roasted vegetables. George McBay ordered another bottle of Sherry and refilled Kate's glass as the musicians started to play in the background.

Kate had another sip of the Sherry. She found herself losing apprehension about the project and was feeling happy for a change.

"You look gorgeous tonight Katie as you always do. Would you like to dance? We've got time for one dance I think. Then we'll go to the taping of the show."

He's holding you too tight, some part of Katie's mind warned her. She shrugged it off. George McBay was a good dancer and she was enjoying being moved around the room in the old-fashioned dance music the band was playing. By the time the band stopped playing Kate realized she was feeling a little tipsy from the Sherry and was glad for the arm George McBay extended as he helped her on with her fancy jacket he had bought before she arrived and led her out to a waiting limousine.

"You don't mind if I kiss you, do you? I can't resist. You look completely gorgeous in that outfit. I've always been attracted to exotic –looking women. And I find the way you argue and stand up to me very invigorating."

Say no, some part of Kate's mind tried to warn her. Instead she made no protest as George McBay gave her a very intimate kiss in the back of the limo. Kate felt her body responding immediately. It had been quite a while since her last failed love affair. She found her body even matching the warmth around her heart that she was receiving.

Watch out, some part of Kate's mind warned her. *You are becoming infatuated.* Kate shook her head in denial. *He's letting me suggest scenes,* she argued.

At the taping of the Aboriginal music show Kate felt herself appreciating the close attention her boss was paying her. The show was wonderful. The collaboration of the musicians creating something new and innovative in the way of Aboriginal music produced spectacular music. The genre was becoming very popular in Canada and the musicians present were some of the very best in the field.

The words of the show's spokesman startled Kate.

"Louis Riel said that my people will sleep for one hundred years and when they awake it will be the artists who give their spirit back."

"Let's hope so," George McBay whispered. "With your help our film can become part of that awakening."

Kate was still feeling the effect of the earlier Sherry. *He's really changed,* she argued with some part of her mind that was still warning her to watch out for this attractive man who was doing a good imitation of some modern version of Doctor Jekyll and Mister Hyde.

Our Spirituality was more explanatory than that of either the Catholic or Protestant missionaries that came amongst us, Kate mused as she listened to one of the musicians singing a song about the other side, the side that we as spirits go to when we die.

"Daddy, leave me the keys to your Cadillac," the musician sang. "You won't need it on the other side."

We were so far ahead in our Spirituality, Kate mused. *Our people always knew about the other side. All the Catholics and Protestant churches talk about is some kind of resurrection from the grave when Jesus returns.*

And these musicians. They are doing the same thing with music that so many of our artists are doing with painting, fabric art and other mediums. You can feel and see the ancient belief systems and world view coming through their art. It is so inspired and creative but you can feel the wisdom of our long-ago ancestors coming through.

Another Sherry?" Kate nodded as George McBay passed her a glass back at his apartment. He had one himself and sat down across from Kate with a notebook in his hand.

"So where do we go from here? With the film?"

"Actually I was wondering where we go from this world when we expire. Our people always believed in a world of spirit. They believed we came into this one in order to learn character development under conditions of materiality. Because our bodies are subject to both physical and mental damage spirits can learn such things as courage and perseverance."

"My father would say that's just superstition but I'm willing to consider your point of view."

Kate was astonished. *George has an open mind,* she decided. *I really like this new George much better.*

"About the film, beautiful?"

Kate struggled to pull her mind back on task. It seemed determined to dwell on the intimate kiss she had shared in the back of the limo.

"We need to explain the significance of the Wampum belt that Pauline Johnson always wore," Kate confided. "The Wampum belts were pictographs that the Iroquois Federation used to capture details of peace treaties and other happenings they made amongst themselves and other tribes. The British adopted the use of the Wampum belts, particularly Sir William Johnson, when he made agreements with the Iroquois. The original Wampum Belt like the one used for the Robinson Treaties had pictographs of equal nations signing peace treaties to share the resources of the land. Those Wampum belts are particularly important now in the present to support the First Nations demands for self-determination and Sovereignty over their lands. The Wampum belts are evidence that originally treaties were signed by the Indians as equal nations possessing Sovereignty and self-determination."

"It will be hard to convince my father of that but I will try."

"We also need to do more scenes of Treaty 7 and 8. Lt. Governor Morris promised a medicine chest and famine relief in order to get the Chiefs to sign Treaty 6. But those promises were not made in Treaty 7 because Morris had been let go for being too extravagant." Kate related that David Laird was not a hero as George's father thought. Kate told George that as the man in charge now Laird stood by when the buffalo disappeared and epidemics surged through the Plains while the Crees and other Plains Indians ate their horses, dogs, anything with buffalo hide in it, and died, the famine was so great.

Kate located one of the history books she had brought with her and showed her boss actual photographs of starving Plains people in front of their tattered tipis. The women were naked on top, lacking clothes of any kind and were shoeless in the surrounding snow. Their children stood beside them looking forlorn. Their bodies were only bones and could be seen in the picture.

"That's terrible, Beautiful. Have another glass of Sherry."

Encouraged, that she was making headway in educating her boss, Kate related how David Laird spent money on stockades rather than rations and it was only when Sitting Bull and five thousand Sioux, escaping the U.S. Calvary after Custer's defeat, made it to the Cypress hills that rations were requested by Laird. He feared that the Plains Indians would join Sitting Bulls' warriors and he would have an Indian war on his hands. The times were so desperate that some Plains Indians even made it all the way to the Peace River Region trying to locate game animals, causing a war with the Indians who occupied that area. Other Plains Indians were cynically given only enough rations to make it to the U.S. where they hunted in vain for the disappeared buffalo.

"The Federal Government was indifferent to the plight of the Plains Indians? That's awful."

"It was more than indifference. Many say that actually a policy of ethnic cleansing was being carried out but I suppose that can't really be proven without a total doubt.

In 1881 after Treaty 7 was negotiated by David Laird, Edward Dewdney, a relative of John A. MacDonald replaced David Laird as Lt. Governor of the North West Territories. He was already Indian Commissioner while Sir John A. was himself the Superintendent-General of Indian Affairs. Sir Cecil Denny, one of the original North West Mounted Police officers was appointed by Dewdney to take over administration of Treaty 7 obligations to seven thousand Indians. Sir Cecil was in charge of the distribution of annuities, seven reserves and two Indian supply Farms.

By 1884 Denny reports in his book "The Law Marches West" that the clause promising Indians the right to travel for hunting and gathering was not being honored. The Indians were restricted to reserves. Denny also reports that by that time Indians were regarded by the growing numbers of settlers and ranchers as "a nuisance and an expense". He reports that the "right of the native red man was not for a moment considered or acknowledged, though more from ignorance than actual hard-heartedness. He was an inferior being to the lordly white man and doomed to pass before advancing civilization" { p. 193}.

The lack of compassion or help for the extreme starvation that followed both the loss of the buffalo and the Tuberculosis striking the Plains people can't be explained just as indifference. It was more than indifference. Failure of any farming activity the natives tried from failed promises for farming instruction, implements and stock plus weather that resulted from the Krakatoa Volcano exploding however succeeded in subjugating the remainder of fierce Plains warriors as well as the Northern ones in time for Treaty 8. Dewdney even ordered Sir Cecil to not supply rations to the starving Indians returning from unsuccessful buffalo hunts over the border, but that Denny did what he could anyway."

"I promise I'll try and get those facts through to my father but it's not going to be easy, Beautiful."

Encouraged further Kate went on to tell George McBay how ironic it was that the very trader who had been responsible for the deaths and degradation of many Plains Indians at Fort Whoop-up by trading particularly virulent fire-water for buffalo robes formed the company I.G. Baker Inc. in Fort Benton, Montana, after the North West Mounted Police shut Fort Whoop-Up down. That firm became very financially successful through supplying third-rate and half-rotten rations to the reserves when the government finally relented and supplied some food relief. It is likely that Superintendent Dewdney also became very rich as a result of the food rations contracts although he had been poor as a church mouse when he arrived to take over Indian Affairs.

Because George McBay seemed so sympathetic Kate went on to tell him how Hayter Reed, one of the Indian Commissioner's after Dewdney even went so far, when some agricultural production was happening at a later date on reserves, to confiscate any of the mechanized equipment that the Indians had managed to procure. He restricted them to primitive digging implements instead and rationalized the move by saying that it would instill better work habits than using modern equipment. Actually his motive was to assure that any Indians on reserves that had managed to grow surplus produce did not compete with the settlers in commercial sales.

Be careful, some part of Kate's mind warned her as her boss continued to listen sympathetically and poured both of them another sherry. *He's very skilled at getting people to think he is in complete empathy with him. His father had him trained as a hard pressure sales person at one point. In the training they instruct salesmen to give full eye contact, and listen carefully and positively to the mark's point of view.*

Nonsense, Kate argued back. *He's wonderful. So understanding, thoughtful, generous and it was so nice of him to get tickets for the taping of that show for me.*

"Let's carry on with the Northern Indians in the Yukon," she suggested. "After David Laird and the other treaty commissioners managed to extract a few signatures for Treaty 8."

"Tell me about it."

Kate felt herself feeling quite tipsy and she faintly recognized infatuation happening again as the handsome man beside her gave her frequent warm eye contact. Another part of her mind was feeding her information about the Yukon Indians who despite being largely left out of the Treaty signing process were considered by Ottawa to have surrendered all rights to their lands.

Kate relayed to Rod how the Chief around Whitehorse, B.C. had in 1902 inquired how they had lost their land without signing any treaties. He was requesting help for his people who were being affected by reduced fur prices. Officials in Ottawa merely promised that the Hudson's Bay Company and the Royal Canadian Mounted Police would not let the natives starve despite the fact that the Hudson's Bay Company had actually been relieved of their responsibility when they sold Rupert's Land. Kate told her boss how In the late 1900's and early twentieth Century the Yukon Indians were decimated by epidemics including Smallpox, Measles, Whooping cough, Tuberculosis and Polio without receiving anything in medical help.

She relayed how later the Department of Indian Affairs took upon itself to control every aspect of the Yukon Indian's lives. Once the Indian Affair's Office members expanded their office from Vancouver to Whitehorse the once independent hunters and gatherers were told where they could live, how their bands were to be organized, where their children would be sent to Residential schools and how much monetary assistance they would get. Even though the Yukon Indians had never signed treaties. She added that instead of being sent to schools closest to home children from many Indian tribes were sent far across the country.

"Children in the Queen Charlotte Islands were sent to Edmonton Alberta, supposedly to learn farming. However the Queen Charlotte Islands have very few places where farming can actually take place. I've seen recent film shots where descendants of the steers placed there by Federal officials roam freely amongst the Indian reserves. They have become pets."

"Those Residential Schools shouldn't be referred to as schools at all. They should be referred to as Brainwashing Institutions. The television personality, Wab Kinew is right, the children who attended them shouldn't be called former students, they should be called survivors."

Kate finally realized she was becoming quite tipsy and refused the refill of Sherry George tried to pour.

"That's unbelievable! How did all this end?"

Kate was astonished by George McBay's unexpected empathy for the plight of the children sent to Residential Schools. He was giving her full eye contact and appeared to be indignant at the Federal Government's arrogance.

Watch out, some part of Kate's mind warned her again. But she disregarded the advice as George McBay continued to give her warm eye contact and full attention.

"We might as well finish this bottle off," he tried again, pouring both of them two more generous portions of the Sherry. Kate swallowed most of hers before continuing. She was feeling quite inebriated but the Sherry was taking away some of the agony she was experiencing as she related the awful history of that time.

"David Laird's haphazard manner of reaching Chiefs during Treaty 8 and even his successor, J.A. McKenna's adhesions to the Treaty the following year backfired on them in the twentieth Century", Kate related. In 1974 the Office of Native Claims had to be created to investigate claims from the many tribes who had never surrendered their lands."

Kate relayed how after having territorial games laws applied to Indians in 1938, having required registration of trap lines in 1950 and becoming aware of their relatives in Alaska making land claims the Yukon Indians formed the Council for Yukon Indians, and launched their own land claims. Kate relayed how in 1968 Elijah Smith, the Chief of the Whitehorse band, demanded a fair settlement for the use of their land as there had been no treaty. That demand as well as the across Canada protest about the White Paper in 1969 resulted in the Office of Native Claims in 1974. In 1980 the Yukon Indians managed an agreement in principle for hunting, fishing, trapping and land-use planning with the Federal Government.

Her words stopped suddenly as George McBay gently pulled her against him and repeated his earlier very intimate kiss. Kate felt her body responding immediately. She did not resist and after several intimate exchanges George picked her up, still embracing her and moved both of them into his bedroom.

"I can't," she managed to protest as her boss gently started undressing her. He placed a condom on himself.

"Why not?" Kate could not for the life of her think of a good reason. Her mind was not functioning properly as a result of the Sherry and infatuation. As George moved himself into the bed and continued his lovemaking Kate gave in to the intensely erotic feelings she was experiencing.

The next morning Kate woke up with a piercing headache and her Sciatica Nerve giving her excruciating pain. It took her a few moments to recall what had happened the night before. She realized she was alone and there was a note on the pillow.

"Thank you for a wonderful night, Beautiful! I've got to go do some urgent business this morning but help yourself to some breakfast and I'll be back as soon as I can. Probably not a good idea to tell Rory anything about last night as we will have to keep secret our mutual attraction from members of the film company.

All my love,

George."

Oh My God, Kate mused. Her mind was immediately assaulted by myriads of conflicting emotions and her head felt like it was being hammered by a jack-hammer. She staggered to her feet ignoring the excruciating pain of her Sciatica Nerve which was flaring painfully.

Rory might be here any minute, some part of her mind warned her. *Your boss is right to not let him realize what happened last night.*

Good advice, Kate decided. She felt completely discombobulated again. *Some part of her mind was telling her she was in love with a wonderful man and another part was telling her that she was on a path to total betrayal of her people.* Memories of the two men with whom she had been deeply in love twice before only to experience the intense pain of loss filled her mind. Kate realized she was experiencing emotion flooding. The intense low self-worth of her childhood and adolescence flooded in on her.

You are the daughter of one of the Aboriginal women who disappeared when you were seven years old, some part of her mind was causing further emotion flooding. *Remember, the police wouldn't even look into the matter for months. Her body was eventually found but no one was ever charged. You are making the same mistake. Trusting some white man.* Kate felt like road kill. *Your grandmother who then raised you would not be pleased at you making this documentary. Thank God she's on the other side.*

Kate forced herself to make it to her feet, swallowed some aspirins she found in George's bathroom and managed to re-make George McBay's bed to almost the way it looked the day before. She limped down the hall, changed into some of her own clothes and, put the used wine glasses into the dishwasher. She managed to find the building's garbage chute for the empty Sherry bottle. Kate returned and collapsed on the sofa overlooking the outside street. Her Sciatica Nerve was raging and she placed a pillow under her left leg hoping it would take the pressure off the nerve.

You are either a fool or a Judas, some part of Kate's mind was outraged. George *McBay is gorgeous, smart and sexy,* another part of her mind argued. *I just want to find love and help my people,* Kate mused. Kate found her heart pounding as her Sciatica Nerve continued to rage. She felt herself going into a total panic.

What if he just wanted to score, some part of her mind questioned. *Maybe he doesn't have any plan to put your suggestions into the documentary. He just wanted to lead you on.*

Oh My God, here's Rory! She could see him getting out of a cab across the street. The doorbell rang minutes later and Kate tried to shut off her fears and tried to look her normal self as Rory came in with his suitcase.

"The scenes look great, you've done a marvelous job of narrating," Kate winced as Rory gave her a friendly hug.

If you only knew what happened last night, Kate thought.

"You know Kate, I've been working on the Quilt Patterns for the Doctrinal Dissertation we are going to do when we have the money from the completed documentary or series of documentaries.

I think we already have the tuition fees for the first year. Have you done any more on your Mosaic Awareness Scale?"

Kate felt another stab of low self- esteem.

Oh My God, Kate instantly felt her stomach nausea increase tenfold and the pain in her head return with a vengeance, *who is the real co-opted person? Rory's been working on his Ph.D. and I've been allowing intimacy with a person with dubious loyalty to First Nations' people.*

"No I haven't," she confessed with much pain. "Tell me about your new quilt patterns."

Kate forced herself to listen carefully to Rory as he pulled out a series of drawings from a portfolio he had brought with him. She forced herself to try and make sense of the first brightly colored quilt pattern Rory concentrated on.

"It is now 1900. The Indian Act is in full force and drastic changes have come to the world views of both Plains and West Coast Indians."

Kate followed Rory's instruction as he pointed to the now tiny Square denoting the influence of what he said was now the size of the influence of the First Nations Square. The Yellow Square was now much smaller than the Red square of WASP influence that represented the world view held by the politicians and capitalists involved with most of the people in government of the new thirty-three year old Dominion of Canada, and the new settlers themselves.

"Indian people are not needed any more by the Dominion of Canada government officials. The country is now no longer threatened by land hungry Americans invading the country and the last of a potential threat to the new settlers, the Blackfoot and Cree warriors, have been subjugated by starvation, epidemics and forced placement in reserves. Their children are being brainwashed in Industrial and Residential Schools that they are inferior to the white, civilized, and Christianized Europeans who now control them. A fairly large green square of Roman Catholic, French speaking people still exists but the rural nature of Quebec is now under assault by capitalists setting up Industrial and Manufacturing endeavors. They are becoming accustomed to wage labor."

Kate could visually see that the Red square people and their WASP world view were now firmly in charge. She went over her knowledge of history of the eighteen eighties to nineteen fifties and grimaced as she remembered the immediate total restriction, humiliation, and even imprisonment of Plains Indians following the subjugation of the Black Feet and Cree from epidemics, famine, and government policy. Rory's words reinforced Kate's pain.

"In the Plains our people were imprisoned on reserves without proper implements to farm or medicines to combat the Tuberculosis and other diseases raging amongst them. Under the Indian Act needless cruelty was done to our children by their forced removal to Industrial and Residential schools with religious teachers who believed their purpose was to take the Indian out of what they believed were subjects much lower in human terms than the indoctrinated individuals of the Catholics, Anglicans, Methodists and Presbyterians they represented. The horrors of the Residential Schools and the cruelty the children experienced have been well documented by the recent "Truth and Reconciliation" hearings and documentaries like "We Were Children.""

Two thirds of the coastal First Nations people in British Columbia had died off because of epidemics and almost all of their lands were being taken by the new settlers. Land developers and forestry companies were rapidly buying the rights to their coastal lands and their forests. B.C. First Nations were left with tiny reserves (ten acres for extended families) that were being made even smaller by the McKenna/ McBride Land Commissioners sent to investigate their complaints but who used the Commission to remove even more good land from the reserves substituting rock piles and low lying, periodically flooding areas instead.

Indian Spiritual beliefs were under full attack. Under Indian Commissioner Duncan Campbell Scott the Sun Dance and the Pot Latch were banned. First Nations people were being hauled off in B.C. to prison for conducting a Pot Latch against orders and their regalia were confiscated and sent to museums. It was not long before the Yellow Square of Plains and B.C. First Nations belief systems were reduced significantly. It was a wonder that that their world views of many centuries survived at all."

"What does the Black Square represent? Though not as large as the red WASP square, those squares are now much larger than the increasingly shrinking, Yellow First Nations one.

"The Black Square represents the American influence of American capitalists investing in the country as well as American settlers who had come in large numbers to take up the offers of cheap but promising farm lands."

Kate somehow managed to force enough of her swirling emotions into the background to review her knowledge of more of the early nineteen hundreds, the time era of Rory's squares.

"North West Mounted Police enforced the Indian Act Restrictions forbidding movement off reserves unless authorized by an Indian Agent. Any First Nations person off a reserve on the Plains began to be stopped and questioned. That must have been the start of the police harassment of First Nations people that became so rampant in Manitoba and Saskatchewan if not elsewhere.

B.C. Indian Chiefs and others were sent to prison after conducting a Potlatch and were humiliated by being told to feed the pigs, the women being strip-searched, and all of them hosed down and fed gruel for food. The artifacts used in the Potlatch were seized and sold, some by the Indian Agent to museums for his own personal gain. Residential school students, moved far from their homes deliberately, were indoctrinated, shown the Catholic pictorial ladder with white Christian people going to Heaven and red-skinned Indian pagans at the bottom burning in Hell not to mention the all to frequent sexual predations by dormitory supervisors and even clergy on occasion."

Kate felt thoroughly depressed, her emotions at an all-time low. Her heart and her stomach felt a deep nausea of humiliation. *Rory's not the one who is co-opted,* some part of her mind told her. *It might be you, if your sudden belief in the changed attitude of George McBay turns out not to be warranted.*

"*I'm suggesting* that we do a linked Ph.D. Dissertation showing the changes and Influence of World Views from Canada's early years to the present day."

Kate felt some release from the all-time low self-worth she seemed to be reaching. She realized that Rory was proposing a very substantial contribution to historical research and analysis of the country's heritage. Despite her swirling emotions she was impressed with the scope of his proposed project.

"That's wonderful, Rory. And I was accusing you of being co-opted. I'm sorry."

"We'll do it together Kate. Let's just hope that the documentary project keeps going long enough to save some more money for the Ph.D. program. I don't have much hope that we will really be allowed to tell the side of First Nations people. George's father will see that the First Nations point of view is edited out even if we do get it into the documentary or documentaries."

"That's why you aren't opposing any of the scenes that George's father wants?"

"Exactly. I want this project to go on as long as possible. I don't have much hope for its success but don't tell George that. He needs to think that he will have a success on his hands, this time. We can take advantage of that hope. He told me once that he had a serious problem with Depression. I told him how my brother had committed suicide when his academic career was halted because of failure to obtain funds. George admitted to me that he understood what had happened to my brother. He told me he also had a history of serious Depression when any of his own projects failed and that if this project didn't succeed he would likely sink again into thoughts of suicide."

Rory's words threw Kate into complete emotional turmoil again.

This is too complicated for me, Kate realized that she had some-how got completely into a very toxic situation. *George McBay has a problem with Depression. I never suspected that he might be men-tally ill. I wonder what was going on with him last night. I thought he was a changed person .*

He's just a highly skilled manipulative person, some part of Kate's mind added a further warning. *He just told Rory that he suffered from Depression to motivate him to try his hardest to make the documentary a success. That can't be true,* Kate argued.

I must at least have changed George's attitudes somewhat towards Indians, Kate allowed herself to hope. *He was listening very atten-tively last night. I have to continue to do that if there's any hope of this documentary or series being balanced. I have to make George see that the film or films would be greatly strengthened by portraying events as they really happened. Or he is going to have a product that can't be sold. Just a tribute to his family's distant relative.*

When George returned several hours later he gave no sign that any serious intimacy had occurred the night before. Kate was experiencing swirling emotions and did not really know what to think.

Later that day Kate sat between George and Rory as his father and George's brother Arthur watched the scene that showed David Laird negotiating Treaty 7 at Blackfoot Crossing. She felt completely discombobulated again by the unexpected turn of events from the day before.

You think you are Cinderella, some part of her mind told her, *but it was the Sherry and the fact that your boss is very manipulative and experienced at seduction. That can't be true,* Kate answered back.

"That actor looks just like cousin David," Chuck McBay boomed. "Quite impressive, with that three piece suit, beard and piercing look. I like the way he managed that treaty without giving away anything but promises, a few dollars, rifles, medals and flags.

"Those words he used, {The Queen wishes to offer you the same as was accepted by the Cree. I do not mean exactly the same terms, but equivalent terms, that will cost the Queen the same amount of money,} that was brilliant. Not exactly the same terms," Kate shuddered as Chuck McBay laughed raucously. "He was taking out the responsibility for paying for schools on reserves, only promising to pay for a teacher. And didn't he remove the clauses for famine relief and medical help. That saved millions in the long run, I remember."

"That treaty gave the Dominion of Canada all of southern Alberta," Kate winced as George McBay elaborated, "including all of the fertile land wanted for the settlers."

"I can't wait for you to film the Treaty 8 scenes," Rod's father sounded really enthusiastic. "That's where David Laird got three quarters of Canada's Central and Northern land area for us including the Tar Sands and the Yukon gold fields for the same terms as in Treaty 7, nearly zilch."

"You need to get a second opinion," Kate rolled her eyes as brother Arthur interfered again. "From someone in the documentary business. This is a very expensive investment. I think your usual good judgment is being undermined by your fondness for our ancestor. Particularly if you decide to fund a series instead of the one documentary praising David Laird."

"Nonsense!" Pain shot through Kate's ears as George's father roared at his younger son. "George has been doing a fine job here this time. I'll advance some more money, George, to underwrite the Treaty 8 scenes. McTavish, that's your name, right, make sure you emphasize how cleverly my ancestor Laird handled those pesky Indians. You can tell from the questions they were asking he didn't have an easy task, even in Treaty 7."

"What about the complete series, Father? I need to pay for the film crews and locations in advance."

"Finish the Treaty 8 scenes first and some from Treaties 9 to 11 where our people secured even more of Canada's land. Then I'll decide whether we'll proceed further. Make sure you keep Kiana, here, I think that's her name, right, narrating the scenes. She's doing a great job. Very emotional. That's working well."

Kate had to dig her nails into her hands again in order not to speak out. She also noted that George McBay was not telling his father that many of the Treaty 8 scenes had already been filmed.

"By the way George," Kate was still listening closely as Chuck McBay suddenly called them back as they were getting up to go. "Your fiancée called me. You had better keep better contact with Rebecca. She's complaining that she hasn't heard from you in weeks and you know how important your marriage is to me. Marrying the heir to the rare metals fortune in Northern Ontario will unite both our businesses."

Kate nearly collapsed to the floor. She could feel her face heat up as it turned bright red. She somehow endured the chatter in the car as Rory and George went over future scenes from Treaties nine to eleven.

He doesn't even seem to care that I now know about his fiancée, the bastard. All he likely wanted was a one-night stand.

Back at the apartment Kate was experiencing a jumble of horrible emotions including extreme low self- worth and humiliation at her own naivety at letting her guard down. George continued to congratulate Rory on the great job he had done getting the scenes his father had viewed together. He was not indicating at all that Kate would be bothered by the news that he had a fiancée named Rebecca.

"We need to continue in this vein. We'll do the Treaties 9 to 11 scenes like Father wants and maybe we should include the rest of British Columbia in this time period as another of father's heroes, Alexander Duncan McRae, was able to make a fortune in 1906 when he to Vancouver to invest in all the new opportunities in resource-rich British Columbia."

Kate tried to pull herself together. She found herself trying to find out if George could even possibly be telling the truth about allowing her to interject some of the real history of her people into the documentary. *He is just highly manipulative,* some part of her brain was trying to tell her. *He is a complete louse,* it added. *You are being taken in by a well-practiced con man totally lacking remorse of any kind.*

That can't be true, another part of Kate's mind still argued back.

"B.C.'s First Nations history is grim," Kate found herself interjecting. "I just read a book by John Muir, a Scots immigrant that came to Victoria, B.C. just after James Douglas had relocated the Hudson's Bay Fort from what became Oregon to Victoria."

"What's grim about that?"

Kate found herself deliberately relating how Douglas was only interested in Hudson's Bay profits, even when he became the first Governor after 1867. She wanted to see how receptive George was to the real history. Kate related that John Muir reported in his autobiography that when three of the miners he was working with complained to Douglas about dangerous work conditions and caused a work stoppage one of Douglas's foremen arranged for the men to be killed by the local Indian tribe. Kate told George and Rory how the Chiefs beheaded the men but Douglas, of course, denied any involvement by his foremen setting the men up. He had a British gun boat strafe the Indian village in retaliation killing many men, women and children.

Kate also related how when smallpox had broken out in Esquimalt near Victoria, Douglas sent the natives visiting back to their villages up the coast which of course resulted in a smallpox epidemic.

"Surely Douglas was aware of the consequences of sending those Indian back instead of placing them under quarantine."

"We certainly don't want to show that scene to my father! Rory what happened to make Alexander Duncan McRae's huge profits in the early nineteen hundreds possible."

See, some part of Kate's mind gloated. *He's not interested at all in anything that will anger his father.* Kate had to dig her nails into her hands again to keep from breaking down in tears from complete humiliation. *You were just a mark* some part of her mind jeered.

"That was due to two huge resources in B.C., the largest Douglas Fir forest in North America, and rivers overflowing with salmon." Kate listened in ever increasing dismay as George McBay looked very pleased at scenes that would please his father. Rory related how McRae had followed the practices of lumbermen in the States and created a monopoly by leasing huge swaths of the Douglas Fir forest from the government for a few cents an acre. Rory then related how McRae had made large contributions to the Government coffers and had the forest leases changed from twenty-five years to perpetuity. Once he had the trees he modernized the forestry industry, creating logging railroads, utilizing spar trees, steam donkeys, steam engines, steam tugs to tow the logs to his huge sawmill in Coquitlam, B.C. and even moved the lumber out on his own ocean-going boats. B.C.'s Douglas Fir forest built the huge colonial empire homes all over the world.

"And the salmon?"

"McRae modernized the salmon industry, too, enlarging the factories and importing the 'Iron Chink' the mechanized fish gutter that replaced lines of gutting crews in the factories."

"That's great Rory, we'll shoot two scenes for my father showing McRae's exploits."

Kate was horrified. George was not showing any attention toward showing the plight of the B.C. natives during the early years. She tried again.

"What about Metlakatla?"

"Metlakatla?"

Kate related how missionaries were brought in to civilize whatever natives remained during and after the smallpox epidemic. She told Rod and Rory how one particular missionary, William Duncan, got some of the Indians near Fort Simpson to relocate with him to a place on the ocean nearby he called Metlakatla by bargaining with the giving of smallpox vaccinations. He only vaccinated Indians who came with him. The natives became Christianized, going as far as having a band and singing Christian hymns in the imitation of an English village Duncan had them build. He even set up English working class cottages, a school, a huge church and a salmon cannery.

However by that time there was a development frenzy happening in B.C. Fort Simpson, being a potential port, was thought to be a lucrative developmental site and the government refused to give the natives title to the land they had built their houses, church, cannery, and school on. Duncan, himself, became so outraged that he relocated the village to Alaska where the U.S. government gave the natives squatting rights on Annette Island. That must have been the one of the very few times that the U. S. Government acted humanitarianly towards Indians."

"We'll shoot the Metlakatla scene later, Katie, I promise. In the meantime Rory I want you to write scripts for the Alexander Duncan McRae scenes. We also need to film some scenes back on the Prairies of the success of the immigration policy of Sir Clifton Sifton. My father thinks highly of bringing all those people onto the Prairies from all over the world. We also need to film some scenes from Treaties 9, 10, 11 so that my father can see how the remaining parts of Canada were surrendered."

"What about the infamous Residential Schools?"

"Yes of course, Katie, thanks. The poet Duncan Campbell Scott was in charge of the Department of Indian Affairs by that time. He is one of my father's heroes. We'll shoot some of those scenes."

Kate found her heart pounding. *Not Duncan Campbell Scott. I can't narrate scenes where he is portrayed as a hero. I don't think George has a problem with Depression, like he told Rory. I think he may be a Multiple Personality or some other serious Personality Disorder. How could he be so sympathetic to the plight of Plains Indians last night and be so insensitive today to the plight of Indians in British Columbia. Maybe it was the Sherry? Maybe I imagined him being sympathetic and understanding.*

At the end of the planning session Kate was jolted further.

"I've had those clothes you will need for publicity packed up in one of my suit cases, Katie, and the travelling case. I want you to take them with you to the airport now ," George instructed. "I've got you and Rory booked for a flight to Ontario. I want you to do a scene from Treaty 9, next where huge northern Ontario areas were surrendered in an adhesion to the Robinson Treaty. There's a car waiting down stairs to take you to the airport."

So that's it, Kate acknowledged in her mind. She found herself almost unable to breathe. *All he wanted was a one-night stand. And those clothes are supposed to pay for it, I expect. He's getting me out of here fast before he likely invites his fiancée.*

Kate was jolted again as Rory left the apartment to take some suitcases downstairs.

"Don't be upset at my having a fiancée, Beautiful" Kate gasped as George McBay seemed to imply that hiding a fiancée was normal procedure for intimacy. "I have no intention of marrying her. It's just that my marriage is the cost that my father is extracting to pay for this documentary. Once the series is funded I can just end the engagement or the marriage for that matter. Rebecca is worth many times what I am. It's you I want to have a lasting relationship with."

Kate found herself completely losing it. *He expects you to co-operate with his complete betrayal,* some part of Kate's mind warned her. *He wants you to join him in completely deceiving his fiancée if really that's what he plans to do.* Kate tried to suppress her emotions at the total lack of integrity that George McBay had just displayed. She tried to express some of her swirling emotions of horror and anger at his words but stopped as Rory came back into the room.

"I'll give you a call later, Katie. I want to give you some directions as to how you narrate about Treaty 8. You both will have to go now to make it to the flight." Kate shuddered inwardly as George McBay rushed both her and Rory out the door.

Thank God we've been assigned separate seats, Katie thought as she and Rory just managed to get on the airplane before it left. *I don't want Rory to see how upset I am.*

Kate recalled George's words. *I'm always attracted to exotic looking women. It's you I want to have a lasting relationship with. My God, he thinks of me as an Indian Princess,* tears flowed down Kate's face. *Like all the postcards of Indian Princesses luring settlers to Canada. Afterwards the same postcards were used to lure tourists during the nineteen thirties and forties. It's like I was told in one of my courses. White men either viewed Indian women as Indian Princesses like Pocahontas or they viewed them as the extremely derogatory name, squaws, the work forces of the Indian village life, nothing in between.* Kate recalled the thousands of postcards generated in the nineteen hundreds on. *Indian Princesses in Birch Bark canoes looking very Caucasian- like but wearing feathers, Buckskins and beads. Or*

Indian women weighed down with beads resembling beasts of burdens carrying wood, etc. in the chores of the villages.

Always the Indian Princesses fell for white explorers like in the movie Pocahontas, she realized. *The real John Smith never even met Pocahontas. We were made into commodities for the propaganda, entertainment and tourist industries.*

Oh My God, George was likely playing out one of those fantasies last night, or who knows, he is so mixed up he likely doesn't even know what he really wants. I am so humiliated. Imagine him speaking of a lasting relationship. Maybe he thinks I will love him forever, be his adoring mistress, putting up with someone else as his dutiful wife, but always available when he decides he needs exotic love.

Negative emotions surged through Kate's mind. She felt completely slimed. *Now I'm one of the endless successions of First Nations women violated by some mixed up white man seeking exotic love. No wonder so many of our young women have disappeared from highways and bars never to be seen again. I feel so wretched. I am so humiliated.*

Kate found herself wondering if she could procure enough sleeping pills somehow to end it all. *Or maybe I can just by a razor and cut my wrists.*

Oh My God! Now I understand why people use Heroin or other drugs to dull the intense pain of humiliation and low self-worth. George likely expects me to me nothing more than a high paid prostitute or maybe even a concubine. Or maybe one night of exotic love is all that he really wanted from me. Perhaps he was just saying those words about a lasting relationship so he could get me out the door before I protested. I should be so lucky. I might never have to see him again.

He said that because he wants you to go on being the narrator of this series, some part of Kate's mind informed her. *He does intend to marry Rebecca. That's his path to wealth and pleasing his father.*

Kate suddenly realized that the man in the seat next to her was looking at her intensely. She suddenly realized that not only was she blotting tears running down her face but she was shaking uncontrollably.

"Sorry," she apologized. "Allergies this time of year. I'm afraid I'm reacting again." Kate somehow managed to stop shaking. She closed her eyes and tried to shut out the intense negative emotions she was experiencing. Instead she found herself dissolving completely into tears. She felt herself shaking violently and starting to sob aloud. *My life never goes the way I want it to,* Kate found herself going into complete despair.

"You need some help, My Dear. I'm a consultant, perhaps I can help you."

Oh My God, Kate forced herself to get some control. *She realized people on the plane were staring in her direction. Thank God Rory is at the back of the plane.*

"A consultant?"

"Yes, a Mental Health consultant for Indian bands."

"I'm sorry. Life has just been too much lately."

"I know. Have you been listening to the Truth and Reconciliation Hearings. So much pain, so much suffering, so much confusion, so many accusations. And for so many decades, over one hundred and thirty years. That's the problem, you know."

"So many decades?"

"Yes. I'm afraid many First Nations people have lost much of their Core Emotional Resiliency."

"Core Emotional Resiliency, whatever is that?"

"The bounce back affect. The ability to live on life's terms. Coming to terms with the fact that life and people won't do what you want. That's likely what you have experienced nearly all your life, like many Indian people."

"That's exactly right." Kate found herself astonished. The man in the next seat was describing her life perfectly. You mean I don't have enough Core Emotional Resiliency."

"Yes. The bounce back affect. You see what the First Nations people experienced, the incredible death rate from European disease, the loss of hunting and gathering territory, which was their way of life, the forced restriction to reserves, the subjugation of the Plains Indians through starvation, disease, imposition of Residential Schools, the intentional destruction of their power, culture and spirituality, and the continuing negative stereotyping from whites around them has diluted the tremendous core emotional resilience that many if not all once had."

"I see what you mean. The cultural, if not actual genocide, the marginalization, the Residential Schools, the poverty and endless stereotyping from the dominant people in Canada, the White, Angle-Saxon Protestants and/or the Roman Catholic French Canadians and the assumptions of both groups of Superiority, has cut the legs out from under the people or even removed them entirely from the Core Emotional Resiliency they had in the past."

"Right. Particularly because the First Nations culture of old was one of looking towards those who came before you. Because of the Brainwashing Institutions, the so-called Residential Schools and the incredible derogatory racism of the settler, clergy and capitalist mentality there have been generation after generation of First Nations people with diluted Core Emotional Resiliency. The Residential School survivors who lived on had very few positive role models to draw from. Many of them were probably suffering from Post-Traumatic Stress Disorder. Stories are coming out like a raid on the kitchen only to return and find one of their own hanging in death as a warning to others and allowing sixteen hours before going after runaways in freezing temperatures."

"But many First Nations people, like me, have become educated. Don't they have more Emotional Core Resiliency."

"Education helps but it is not the panacea it is perceived to be. So you have the ability through education to organize an economic structure but you still don't have the emotional resiliency coping skills you need. So when things get tough you collapse into despair and hopelessness, turn to addiction or suicide ideation, thoughts of "I don't have any control over my life."

"That's exactly what I have been experiencing throughout my own life."

"Yes. Because of Ethno-Centric Monoculturalism if not outright Racism it is even more challenging to live out life as an aboriginal person because you are experiencing discrimination and prejudice placed on you always. Because you come to every social interaction concerned about what people think of you. Within a marginalized population even if you do prove yourself you are often labelled as a "come up again", an Irish term that means that you think you are better than everyone else."

"A come up again?"

"Yes, I think the First Nations term is Chugs, an unfortunate labeling where First Nations people take on the attitudes of the aggressor. This results in a kind of overwhelm – with all the challenges facing them many First Nations people don't even get out of the starting gate."

"What's the answer to all this incredible negativity?"

The culture is actually correct to look to those who came before for role models but it is helpful to look in two places, before and after the one hundred and thirty years of residential school

victimization. Perhaps to go back to heroes like Tecumseh and
to present day, positive First Nations Role models.

"Tecumseh?"

"Yes, the chief who joined forces with British General Sir
Isaac Brock, and used his strategic battle knowledge to fool the
thousands of American troops waiting to invade Canada in the
War of 1812 into thinking that several hundred Indian and
British defenders were numbered into the thousands."

"How did he do that?"

"The American invaders were across the Detroit River.
Tecumseh had his natives go in circles continuously through open-
ings in the woods that could be viewed. The American thought
they were viewing thousands rather than hundreds of both natives and soldiers. Then Tecumseh and Brock decided to attack,
an audacious move. The Americans, terrified of the Natives, ran
and suffered the most humiliating defeat. Talking about thinking outside of the box, that was an example of Core Emotional
Resiliency, and showed how innovative our people can be. Instead
of mourning the Indian Country that had already been stolen from
his people and falling into despair Tecumseh fought back and de-
layed the process for a while."

"Our people?"

"Yes, I'm part Cree and part French. My people, as you know,
received the derogatory label Half-breeds, and now call themselves Metis. We are proud now of our combination Aboriginal-
French, or Aboriginal-British heritage." Kate looked closely at
the man's features. She could see that he was part First Nations.

"I'm Kate Golden Eagle," Kate held out her hand.

"Pleased to meet you Kate, I'm Luke Spencer."

"Dr. Luke Spencer?"

"Yes. As you know Metis people likely suffered even more than people lucky enough to be considered Indians by the Treaty makers back in the late eighteen hundreds and early nineteen hundreds."

"They did? At least the Metis children didn't have to attend Residential Schools."

"Some of us did. There was a lot of confusion about who were Metis people and who were Indians. But it was when the Dominion of Canada was formed in 1867 that Metis people were left out of the people who were given land. Metis people had already been forced west out of Upper Canada from the discrimination by the WASP settlers. We even formed a Provisional Government under Louis Riel and Gabriel Dumont but the Dominion of Canada government refused to negotiate with us. We fought but after our defeat at Batouche when Sir John A. brought in thousands of soldiers, we became pariahs. At Batouche we ran out of ammunition, fled and our survivors became a landless people."

"Landless?"

"Yes. We were forced to live on road allowances, and squat on undeveloped Crown land from which we were forcibly removed when the endless wave of European settlers kept coming."

"Why were you worse off than First Nations' people?"

"They at least had some land in reserves, however inadequate the land was, and eventually some rations were supplied. We had nothing. We were forced to take whatever marginal jobs we could find from settlers to survive, usually the back breaking labor of pulling rocks and stumps. We were forced to build mud shacks on squatted land for our families, and eat roots, gophers and berries. Our fathers managed to gain some money by trapping but by that time many used alcohol to deaden the pain of poverty and hopelessness. My grandmother told me tales of eating lard, bannock and gophers for lunch at school while settler children looked on in derision. They sat on one side of the school while we sat on the other. My grandmother told me how Metis school children had to learn how to fight to protect themselves."

"Doesn't being called doctor help now?"

"Yes, but you have to realize that many of both your and my people, even with higher degrees, are functioning with trauma brains because of the high rates of suicide and addiction in our extended families and in many of the urban centers where Metis, non-Status Indians and Status Indians and their children who have moved to the cities have grown up in marginalized circumstances with put-downs from the non-Indigenous people around them including many teachers and authority figures."

"Trauma brains?"

"Yes, they are constantly emotionally flooding out. Their limbic systems fire as they are triggering off everything. They are still being overwhelmed with prejudice, and overwhelmed with their own family and friend tragedies. Where I was living in the slums there were suicides after suicides and the rate of violence against women was staggering."

"It's the same on some of our reserves. What is the answer to all this?"

"Because the cultural transmission of Core Emotional Resiliency from our Role Models of old was massively interrupted by dislocation, death, racism, poverty, starvation, cultural genocide and ethnic cleansing of the Plains, it is necessary to find new role models and rebuild paths to strong Core Emotional Resiliency."

"What would be some of the ways to do that?"

"We need to look at past Indian and Pan-Indian role models. People of Color like Nelson Mandela, Martin Luther King are excellent role models. Chief Pontiac who tried to pull together a united tribal effort to stop the invading, Imperialistic, white people is another role model. So is Chief Tecumseh who stopped the myriads of American invaders, at least for a while. A wonderful female role model is Pauline Johnson who demonstrated core Emotional Resiliency. Despite being female and part- aboriginal she never stopped writing and speaking poems and prose of pride of her father's race and injustice to them.

As far as people of mixed Aboriginal/European ancestry like me are concerned, we often become powerful role models for others. Herb Kane and Bill Reid are excellent examples. Bill Reid almost single-handedly revived the Haida traditional art works while Herb Kane, a part Hawaiian, almost single-handedly started the Hawaiian Renaissance with his portraits of ancient Hawaiians and his recreation of the voyaging canoe Hokule'a. These are just a few examples of possible role models."

"And the Trauma Brain. How do we combat that?"

"The process of forgiveness involves releasing from the emotional prison of resentment. Forgiveness is a gift we give ourselves. If you don't forgive you don't take back your power over your own life. You are handing that power to someone else."

"And?"

"You have to take the responsibility of not moving forward, of not taking that terrible experience or experiences as life lessons in character development. You have to validate the character you have developed even if only to survive this far. You need lessons in character development to prepare for the next chapter in life, to take your life to the next emotional level. If you stay stuck and life passes by you are actively feeling the same overwhelm that is unfortunately culturally around in many reserves or urban slums. That overwhelm becomes a vicious circle. Blame to overwhelm to despair to hopelessness to addiction to even homelessness and/or suicide. It undermines whatever core emotional resiliency you possess. You never step into freedom."

"So to use a metaphor. Life is a stream moving forward. To go down the stream with a canoe as Pauline Johnson often did, sometimes you have to go with the current not hide out in a back water. And there are rocks you must cope with and rapids."

"Exactly, think of the oyster. Sand is inserted into its shell. The oyster needs the friction of the sand to make the pearl. The oyster can't just give up. You can't grow into your power and potential of who you are supposed to be without adversity. To use another metaphor, everyone is waiting for the great canoe that is carrying others. You want to join, but sometimes there is no one else in the canoe. You have to step up and be the first person to paddle and guide the canoe. It might be a while before someone else turns up."

"We are in a cultural crisis. Those who have become before us are grieving. It is appropriate for us to help them in their grieving. However there is now a crisis of conscience on some of our reserves and in our urban slums. We must go beyond this. We must set our own value. We no longer should make excuses for poor behavior. We should no longer silently tolerate the poor behavior that so many toxic relationships role model. We must not harbor the sexual predator even if he, or his father did attend a Residential School. We must fall in love with the potential that people can be. We must hold out for better things. Instead of waiting for your Prince or Princess to come, fueled by a make-up-break-up cycle that does produce excitement of intensity but destroys everyone including children in the process, we must set our own value. People will come and meet you in the value you set for yourself.

Resiliency, the ability to unhook from situations that are unhealthy, the strength to shift curves that come in your life must be developed. Don't say, I don't deserve this moment, poor me, why did someone treat me like that. Above all take personal responsibility for your actions. Borrow Barack Obama's great oratory ability, borrow Gandhi's compassion, Mandala's determination, King's outspokenness, Churchill's courage, Pauline Johnson's spirit of being a powerful woman role model, borrow from those who have gone before you as global community models. It's really all about the journey. Ask if you have the strength and resiliency to step into that canoe, to assert yourself as a member of a more positive community that might even not even exist yet. Capture the vision of where you are going no matter what you currently might be going through."

Kate could feel shivers going through her at Luke Spencer's words. She could feel her trauma brain trying to cycle again and forced herself to suppress the low self-worth it was trying to induce.

You've had another lesson in the necessity to develop emotional intimacy before allowing sexual intimacy, some part of Kate's mind told her. *Take responsibility for your mistake in allowing George McBay to take advantage of you. Don't go on blaming him. Look at the whole experience as a learning lesson.*

"You know, non-First Nations Canadians could learn from the model you have just proposed too. Many of them are sinking into addiction and hopelessness as well."

"Exactly my Dear! They should learn to step up to a new canoe as well. After all we are all in the same canoe, one whose parameters contain all that we have and know on this planet. Innovation, compassion and following the ways of the few role models who have become the best that they can be are the name of the game right now."

"Thank you so much Luke. You've given me a new way to look at failure and disappointment. I promise I'll try and boost my level of Core Emotional Resiliency. It may take a while but I'll make a conscious effort to do so."

Silence ensued as Luke nodded and proceeded to read the book he had been trying to read. Kate went over the events of the past few months in her mind.

You have to go on with this travesty, Kate was amazed to find some part of her mind addressing her. *Rory is right. You need the money to do a Ph.D. or at least to start one. Get started and you might be able to be a Teaching Assistant to finance the rest. That way you and he will be able to counter some of the propaganda against First Nations written in the history texts from way back. Or even be able to launch an attack on the negative stereotypes of First Nations people, particularly women, so persuasive in Canadian society. Maybe we might be able to get the facts of what happened to both aboriginal and Metis people out in the open.*

Maybe Rory and I will get a chance to put some scenes of resiliency into this documentary, Kate thought as she struggled to regain some balance in her life. *I'll pretend to go along and watch for an opportunity. Luke spencer is right. I don't need a re-enactment of the kind of toxic relationship George McBay is likely setting up for me. I imagine he expects me to be the narrator of his documentaries by doubling as his adoring mistress anytime he wants exotic love.*

Sometimes you do need to step into the canoe yourself, Kate thought, recalling Luke Spencer's words. *There are some people who have done so. Names came into Kate's mind. MaryEllen Turpel Lafond, the B. C.*

Children's Advocate who didn't hesitate to criticize millions of dollars transferred to Aboriginal Communities for child welfare that don't seem to have reached or helped the recipients due to vested interest or funds diverted elsewhere or not being received in the first place.

Judge Murray Sinclair who tells educational facilities for both Aboriginals children and non-Aboriginal children that they need to teach respect between cultures. Nellie Cournoyea, the part Inupiaq child who went on to educate herself by taking correspondence courses sent to her family's bush camp and went on to be the sixth Premier of the North West Territories and the Chair and CEO of the Inuvialuit Regional Corporation. Nellie tells her people to dream bigger dreams and opening the window onto a world of possibilities and always to be a servant to their people.

And talk about stepping into a canoe. What about a boat, the Odeyak, that didn't even exist before a community built it. The innovative, twenty-six foot part kayak, part canoe vessel, that the villagers of two tiny communities in Northern Quebec on the Great Whale River used to stop Hydro-Quebec in its tracks. Kate felt herself losing some of the nauseating gut feelings of low self- worth as she recalled the great victory of the Cree and Inuit people over both the Nationalism of Quebecers and greedy politicians who were going to finance Quebecers aspirations of an Independent Nation with billions through exporting power to Vermont. The government officials and capitalists had thought nothing of ending the way of life for the Cree village of Whapmagoostui and the Inuit village of Kuujjuaraapik in the 1990's by without asking or negotiating doubling or tripling the area flooded already by the James Bay agreement.

Those sixty villagers, many of whom had never been out of the remote area, built the Odeyak and took it first by dogsled across hundreds of miles until the Great Whale River thawed enough to launch it. Then they paddled in groups of ten down the swift currents to the St. Lawrence River, then to the Hudson River in time to join Pete Seeger and the Environmental Groups on Earth Day in 1990 to publicize their plight and beg the people of Vermont not to sign the contract with Hydro-Quebec that would seal their fates forever by the flooding of their trap lines, food gathering and hunting areas. The fact that the people of the canoe/ kayak were successful was astounding.

What a louse, Kate thought of her humiliation again. *George McBay probably uses the same technique on all the women he decides to seduce. I'll have to protect myself if I'm unfortunate enough to be in his presence again, make sure I'm never alone.*

Chapter 6. Treaties 9 to 11.

Several days later Katie was forced to view an actor portraying Duncan Campbell Scott, one of the Treaty 9 Commissioners as he, in 1904, along with another Indian Affairs official, Samuel Stewart and a miner, named D. G. MacMartin, representing the province of Ontario, separated extremely valuable, unextinguished lands in Northern Ontario from their rightful owners. It was known that the lands contained gold, silver and valuable base metals.

"Boy did they ever pick those commissioners, Kate mused. Duncan Campbell Scott, the Indian's worst nightmare, a lackey of his from the Bureau of Indian Affairs and someone from the Mining Industry who would benefit from acquiring lands containing valuable minerals. She listened closely to the words that Rory had written. Promises were made orally to not restrict in any manner the hunting and fishing rights of the Indians. Promises of medical help were insinuated by the presence of a doctor with the Treaty Commissioners and Red Coated Dominion Police Force likely reminded the natives of the power that had been demonstrated by the eight thousand troops sent in to end the Riel Rebellion.

Those promises were never put in the written treaty, Kate mused sadly, *and the remuneration given was pretty close to what had been given over fifty years previously during other Treaties, twelve dollars initially followed by four dollars annually. Imagine what those mining leases brought in for both the Federal and Provincial Governments, Billions over the years.*

Dressed in buckskins as Pauline Johnson, Kate somehow managed to force herself to repeat Chief Missabay's words of thanks for the travesty that had been conducted.

That should please Chuck McBay no end, she mused bitterly at the recreated feast scene after the signing. Kate could not bring herself to eat any of the food provided. She was still experiencing extremely low self-worth at allowing her delusional thinking concerning George McBay.

I'm going to go on with this travesty, Kate reminded herself. She remembered the decision in the airplane. *I need at least to start that Ph.D. I need it to put a dent at least into the unconscious belief system of so many non-Indigenous Canadians that First Nation's people are losers and takers. The real takers are the officials of the Dominion of Canada and the Capitalists without social responsibility that received the valuable timber and minerals in Indian lands for a song.*

A week later, Kate found herself in Northern Saskatchewan watching another actor portray veteran Commissioner J. A. McKenna who in 1906 under Treaty 10 extracted extinguishment of another eighty-five thousand square miles east of Treaty 8 surrendered lands. Again she heard promises orally for provision of medicine and hunting rights that were never placed in the written treaty.

Two weeks later Kate watched the recreation of treaty 11 talks in 1921, where three hundred and seventy two thousand square miles east of the Yukon Territory and south of the Arctic Ocean were exchanged in haste after oil was discovered in Norman Wells.

The historian, J.R. Miller in his book "Compact, Contract, Covenant" was right, Kate mused, *when he said: "In the North, it was clear that in gaining an 'empire', Canada was ever more clearly acting like an oppressive colonizer* (p. 221). Kate found herself sighing deeply in despair at the same remuneration $12 initially, and $5 annually, even at this late date.

Of course the red coated R.C.M.P., the missionaries and a doctor were involved again in being present when this treaty took place, Kate sighed. *The Hudson's Bay Company also provided transportation for the Treaty party again.* She couldn't eat any of the food at the feast provided either.

"What now?" Kate asked Rory as they packed up from the Treaty 11 shots. "And what's happened to George McBay? We haven't seen him since the last Vancouver trip."

"Oddly enough, George has advanced some money to do some more shots of modern day conditions for First Nations across Canada who have negotiated or are negotiating modern treaties. He said that his father has still not agreed to make the documentary into a series but wants to see these possible scenes for the documentary made. George e-mailed directions to Bill Mason and me yesterday. Apparently he's in the midst of marriage preparations with his fiancée and can't join us himself."

Kate lurched as she felt a gut-wrenching nausea at Rory's words. *So he was outright lying to me,* Kate acknowledged. She fought to keep her extreme emotional flare up from Rory. *You are so lucky,* some part of her mind told her. *That man is extremely mixed up, likely mentally ill or at least suffering from some type of Personality Disorder. You could have spent years being manipulated in extremely toxic circumstances. Now you can just ignore him, even if he contacts you.*

"What are his new directions?" Kate managed to keep her nausea under control. *I'll deal with this later,* she promised herself.

"George wants Bill and me to do a quick tour with you as Pauline Johnson, of course, and film some scenes of

First Nations communities across Canada who've managed to negotiate modern treaties or have adopted entrepreneur ways to try and further their economic well- being. George says that we should show that those treaties are a complete waste of time.

"A complete waste of time?"

"Apparently another of George's father's hero's is Melvin H. Smith, the author of the book {Our Home or Native Land?} George's father wants us to record the jurisdictional chaos and financial waste that the author is sure is already resulting from those treaties."

Kate gulped deeply. Rory's words came back. *George McBay is getting married. That must have been the price his father extracted for financing the documentary,* Kate mused. She could feel her face going beet red with humiliation. *Maybe his father gave him an ultimatum like marry Rebecca or I won't even finance the rest of this documentary,* some part of Kate's mind tried to offer excuses for George McBay. Kate sighed deeply as she realized that some part of her unconscious mind, she was still hoping that George had been truthful when he told her that she was the one he really wanted to have a lasting relationship with. Nausea and Sciatica pain completely overtook her at that acknowledgement.

"This will give me an opportunity to update my World View Quilt patterns," Kate managed to keep from showing the enormous reaction she was experiencing at Rory's news. "I'm trying to evaluate how much influence First Nations have now on the Canadian scene."

"What about portraying these treaties as failures? I'm sure that's not true at all. I refuse to narrate any more lies about the truth of colonization and the truth about actual progress First Nations are making with modern self-government treaties."

"Just carry on for a little longer Kate. We have to get as much money towards our Ph.D.'s as possible. George warned Bill Mason that we really need to please his father with these scenes. He says he's threatening to withhold any more funds unless we really show how great the Canadian Government has been to First Nations since Confederation."

Kate felt her Sciatica pain flaring intensely.

"I don't think I can cope with either of the McBay's any longer. You know the truth. Confederation was when the government of the myriads of Orange Irish Protestants that had been brought over and other white immigrants with a Superiority complex decided to totally disinherit the rightful owners of the land. They had no intention of sharing the resources like our Chiefs believed." Kate felt overwhelmed by emotion. "I'm tempted to send in my resignation. It's like we are hostages in an extortion threat. Portray Canadian actions at Confederation as well meaning and noble or you won't even get enough money to finish the one documentary."

"A few more weeks and we will know for sure if we have a documentary or a series."

Kate felt totally emotionally drained. She felt she needed to argue with Rory this time.

"What if Chuck McBay doesn't finance the series Rory? But goes ahead with this documentary. You and I are going to be responsible for a documentary praising the very people that gained an Empire for pennies and placed our people into hopeless conditions on reserves and our children into Brainwashing Institutions for one hundred and thirty years."

"Just a little longer Kate. We should know soon anyway."

He's just trying to succeed where his brother failed," some part of her mind told her.

"I guess I have no choice. Maybe it will only be for a few more weeks. I hope so. I'm totally losing faith that we can put any balance in this documentary," Kate managed. "Where are we going first?"

"To British Columbia. That's where most of the modern day treaties have been negotiated."

"That's because British officials were so cheap they told James Douglas to stop making treaties with B. C.'s indians. He only negotiated fourteen on Vancouver Island. I guess the blankets he was giving them were breaking the Bank of England. And then government after government in British Columbia, except for the brief reign of the New Democratic Party, refused to acknowledge Aboriginal Title. Now it is likely going to cost a fortune to negotiate extinguishment. Have you got some say over the places we are going to visit?"

"Yes, oddly enough. George seems to have stopped his micro-management now that's he's so busy into his marriage preparations."

"You know that Frank Calder and James Gosnell, from B.C. represent good examples of modern day role models of Core Emotional Resiliency."

"Core Emotional Resiliency, whatever is that?"

"The Bounce-Back Effect," Kate repeated Luke Spencer's words. "The ability to keep bouncing back from negative experiences that have likely even caused Post Traumatic Stress Disorder in generations of Residential School survivors. Or with many of our people who have experienced and are still experiencing the suicides, addiction and violence against women from marginalization on our reserves and stereotyping/discrimination in urban settings."

"Oh, you mean that despite the fact that Calder and Gosnell attended Residential Schools they didn't cave in to hopelessness. They took the actual knowledge they learned, furthered it and used it to attack the Indian Act itself. Those two and others like them have persevered and their efforts have resulted in modern-day treaties with some self-government features."

"Exactly. Why don't we visit the places where Gosnell and others have negotiated self-government treaties?"

"I've got Billy Mason setting up for scenes in the Okanagan. You know, the Westbank First Nations. They seem to be functioning well, at least economically."

"You know that Chuck McBay is looking for scenes of failure not success."

"I know," Kate smiled as Rory seemed to contemplate her words. His next words really astonished her.

"Maybe it is our time to get even, to set the facts straight. I really suspect that you are right. I don't really think George's father is going to finance anything much more anyway. I think that's why George hasn't been directing things on the spot himself. Maybe we should shoot some scenes that will send his father through the roof. We've probably got enough saved for the start of our Ph.D.'s anyway."

Kate felt some of her heavy emotion lift. "I like what you are saying now. You know if Chuck McBay isn't going to finance a series, we are going to be stuck with a documentary applauding the appalling actions of Dominion of Government members determined to get an Empire for a song and Indian Affairs Officials who like Duncan Campbell Scott were obsessed with ending what they viewed as the Indian problem by taking the Indian out of the Indian."

A week later Kate found herself, dressed in the Pauline Johnson costume, staring at the headquarters of the Westbank First Nation's government. It was inside a modern office building beside a busy street where myriads of businesses paid leases to the Westbank First Nation. Bill Mason had already shot scenes of the prosperity that had come to the Westbank Nation after it had successfully negotiated a partial, self-government treaty that had been given Royal Assent under Bill C-11 in Ottawa on May 6, 2004. The Westbank First Nation band had freed themselves from some of the control of Government officials under the Indian Act.

Kate had been amazed at the expansion of the reserve and the resulting leases and economic activity including several modern subdivisions, a golf course, the Westbank Hub Centre containing many businesses including Canadian Tire, and several High rises, with the land leased from the Indian Band. The Westbank Nation management also had Day Care and Health Services under their control.

"The members of the Westbank First Nation made a decision to change their circumstances," Kate narrated as Rory smiled. "They broke away from the Okanagan Indian Band, and won the battle to charge Property Tax to non-Indigenous people living on their reserve. After winning a court case against several families of non-Indigenous people living on their lands and negotiating a three thousand acre expansion to their land they have incredibly improved their economic and other living conditions.

This is an example somewhat like what was visualized by Indian Chiefs in even the earliest of peace treaties recorded by Indians in the original Two Row Wampum Belt. The two rows symbolized Indian warriors in canoes and Europeans in their boats, side-by-side, but separate going down a river. In other words,"

Kate narrated, "the Indians had the vision that both groups, themselves and the Europeans who had come to their lands, would have control of each of their boats but not of each other's vehicles. They would share the resources together.

That's what these modern treaties are starting to resemble. Treaties that allow First Nations Communities to control their own economic and cultural destiny. Much of the Westbank Nation's success is because of their ability to allow faster access to leases and development proposals than other types of Government and private company arrangements. They don't have to wait until officials of the Northern Development and Indian Affairs Department make a decision.

Finally the Supreme Court of Canada is recognizing Aboriginal Title to land in B.C. Kate found herself narrating. On June 28th, 2014 the Tsilhqot'in Nation had aboriginal title declared from the Supreme Court of Canada over one thousand seven hundred fifty square kilometers on the West side of the Fraser River in the Chilcotin region of British Columbia. This is the first time that Aboriginal Title has been declared over the ground in B.C. The Tsilhqot'in Nation have been given the right not just to be consulted on developments in their lands but the right of consent.

They have also had declaration of their ownership, under Unextinguished Title to more than the five or eight percent of their claimed land base that the B.C. Treaty Commission has been allowing. This case also sets precedents for other land in Canada that was not extinguished by Treaty. In the words of Bill Gallagher, in Northern Ontario Business, June 30, 2014, In the Maritimes and parts of Quebec the British Crown's Peace and Friendship Treaties do not include the "cede, release and surrender" provision. The Supreme Court has already ruled that the Aboriginal title question has not been resolved in that area.]

Kate noticed Bill Mason looking extremely uncomfortable as she ended the script written by Rory.

"Chuck McBay is not going to like that last paragraph. And what about problems that have arisen with this Westbank Nation Treaty?"

"I couldn't find any," Kate smiled as Rory answered. "I did a review of the literature but nothing was available. Several non-Indian families living on Westbank Nation lands protested to the courts of having Indigenous control over them but lost in Court."

"Maybe this is going well because Kelowna, where the Westbank First Nation is located, in the Okanagan has been a rapidly, developing area, development that was aided by the construction of the Coquihalla highway that connects the Okanagan with Vancouver."

"Perhaps, let's go to the far north of B. C. next. Where the Nisga'a Treaty was negotiated .

A week later Kate found herself in front of the impressive Nisga'a Government building, an impressive structure resembling a modern version of a long house. Inside she watched as all members of the Nisga'a government including representatives from the Youth Council, the Elder's Council and the four Nisga'a villages discussed relevant changes to their laws. Fee simple ownership of house and land was recently allowed to happen by the Nisga'a Government in order for people with businesses like Bed and Breakfast facilities to obtain mortgages.

Kate was relieved that the community would not lose these lands through any default on the mortgages, the balance owing would be paid by the band, unlike the allotment system in the

United States that for many years was used to remove reserve land when allotment owners were allowed to sell to non-Indians. Most of the American Indians were in total poverty and the temptation to sell the land allotments was overwhelming. The allotment system in the U.S. resulted in eighty percent of reserve land being removed from the reserves before it was repealed.

Kate was astonished that the folks sitting next to her turned out to be visiting government officials from Norway who were consulting with the Nisga'a people about appropriate ways to govern and interact with Indigenous people in their country, the Reindeer herding people in the North of Norway.

Later that day Kate viewed a scene in the Nisga'a High School where graduates were preparing to move on to College and University opportunities. Nisga'a regalia was everywhere as well as Nisga'a Totem Poles and ceremonies. Although the Village did not have sufficient funds for all graduates to move on they financed all they could. Kate was amazed that more than thirty-seven university degrees were already in the hands of the adults in the Village community. The Nisga'a Fisheries were being carefully monitored by the band. Modern equipment measuring the numbers of salmon in the Nass River was utilized while each year a small number of fishing days for the residents gave them a catch of six hundred salmon each, with some sales of the fish being allowed.

Kate narrated later as Pauline Johnson that it was obvious that the Nisga'a community had benefitted from the self-government Treaty they had negotiated with so much difficulty for thirteen long years.

"The people of the Nass Valley are indeed headed down a very bright path," she concluded. "They have established literacy, numeracy, language and culture through their control of the

Education system on their lands. Pride in their culture by members of all ages is fully evident and they do not hesitate to show it off to the many tourists coming for the myriads of activities evident in the four Nisga'a villages and surrounding areas like Terrace and Prince Rupert. Their graduating students are determined to obtain degrees in subjects valuable for their resource and community development and return to their villages."

"There must be somewhere that there is jurisdictional chaos and financial ruin as a result of these treaties," Kate and Rory looked at each other as Bill Mason complained.

"Some members of the community are complaining about having to pay Property and Income Tax," Rory countered. "That was agreed to start in 2012 and now people have to include that in their budgets. Some of the money is returned to the Nisga'a government though to pay government expenses."

"Chuck McBay would not consider that a problem," Bill Mason commented. "Unless the part of the tax money that was returned to the Nisga'a."

"Trap line jurisdiction is still under the Provincial Government," Rory added.

"Chuck McBay wouldn't consider that a problem either. Kate thought that Bill Mason sounded really worried.

"Let's try Cranbrook, B.C.," Rory suggested. "The First Nations there obtained a treaty and had the audacity to re-build their huge Residential School into a Luxury Resort and Golf Resort instead of just tearing it down as many wanted to do."

"Good," Kate could see that Bill Mason was somewhat placated at Rory's suggestion. "Surely they must have run into financial problems at least with that project."

Several days later Kate found herself dressed as Pauline Johnson holding a golf driver on the tee of the first hole of an eighteen hole golf course five minutes by shuttle from the Cranbrook International Airport.

'Welcome to the St. Eugene Mission Resort," she narrated. The Ktunaxa First Nation, during a 1993 Treaty negotiation process took a chance. They decided to turn their stone, historic, Residential School into a luxury Resort. The Residential School had from 1912 to 1970 indoctrinated rather than educated five thousand First Nation children. It took ten years and forty million dollars to turn the building into a Hotel with one hundred twenty five rooms, a casino, four restaurants, meeting rooms, a recreation center and an eighteen hole golf course.

The Resort now has a 2014 Certificate of Excellence from Trip Advisor and employs over two hundred people year round, three hundred in the summer. A plaque inside the building holds the words of Indian Band Chief Sophie Pierre that says [Since it was within the St. Eugene Mission School that the culture of the Kootenay Indians was taken away, it should be within the building that it is returned.] How is that for long overdue justice? What a tribute to Core Emotional Resiliency."

"Surely there are some problems with this project?" Bill Mason insisted.

"I don't think so," Kate smiled as Rory replied. "In 2004 the Ktunaxa Nation partnered with the neighboring Samson Cree Nation in Alberta and the Mnjikming Nation in Ontario. Now an Interpretive Center stands beside the Resort and contemporary Aboriginal Art is displayed, Elders share local legends and history and traditional foods are served in the Hotel restaurant. The Yagan Nukly Traditional Pow Wow is held here every year."

"Let's go to Tsawassen," Bill Mason suggested. "We have to find some disasters for Chuck McBay or he is not going to give his son further funding. What about Indian problems in urban centers?" Kate reeled as Bill Mason blustered. "There doesn't seem to have been much done by First Nations Treaties to ameliorate conditions for Indians in Canada's cities."

"That's because under the Indian Act over sixty percent of Canada's Indigenous people are legally (according to Indian Act rules) non-status. The non-status Indians compose the majority of Aboriginal people in big city centers. First Nations Bands do not receive funds for Non-Status Indians."

"What do you mean?"

"From the start of the Indian Act the government has tried to keep the number of Status Indians it was responsible for down as low as possible. To do that Metis people were not given title to land they were living on. Under treaties the Half-Breed Script Commissioners, that accompanied the Treaty Commissioners, Metis people were only given script for land but to find and register land they would have had to travel hundreds of miles to registry offices. Most of them sold the script to speculators for very little as was expected by even Treaty officials.

The speculators then flipped the script to settlers or others wanting to make a quick profit. As a result the government avoided a land base for Metis people. Add to that the numbers of Indians who have lost status through what was called enfranchisement and females who lost status by marrying white men until 1978, there are a large number of Aboriginal or part Aboriginal people eliminated by the Indian Act requirements for membership in First Nation Bands."

"What are you talking about? Those Natives in Urban areas just had the sense to move away from tiny communities in rural areas that they could not see a future in."

"No Bill, the enfranchisement (meaning the forced assimilation of Indigenous people in Canada) and dis-allowance or removal from the Band lists was carefully planned by the settler ministers of the Dominion of Canada."

Kate was astounded at Rory now joining her in telling the real story of what happened to Indigenous people in Canada. She had experienced the extremely problematic task of what she now knew that psychologist Erik Erikson called the Adolescent Identity Achievement task (who am I and what am I going to do with my life) when she was a teenager. Her mother had been removed from her Band Council list when her father, a full-blooded Mohawk, died. Her mother who had come from a Cree community did not qualify for full status under her own right under the Indian Act because her own mother had been married to a non-status Indian.

Kate found her Amygdala firing as she re-lived being forced from her reserve community, her mother's move to slums in Calgary, the loss of close friends and the horrible discrimination she experienced from the white teachers and white students when she was placed in a white school. *I didn't feel I belonged anywhere,* Kate remembered. We were in total poverty. I remember the cockroaches we could never get rid of, the ill-fitting clothes, the hungry feeling when my mother couldn't even put much food on the table, and one of my sisters nearly dying from an ear infection when money was not available for the anti-biotic she needed.

Even now, *when I visit people I used to know on the reserve they insinuate that I am not a real Indian. In Urban settings, my friends who are mainly not Status Indians are forever trying to decide whether people who join them are real Indian, Metis or even just white wanna-bees. And when my friends or other Indigenous people recognize me as the narrator of this documentary that is portraying a white, Ethno-Centric, Monoculturalist view of Canadian history I am going to be shunned.*

Later when Bill Mason filmed her as Pauline Johnson in front of the many industrial cranes building the new, huge Shopping Centers of the Tsawwassen First Nation Kate experienced gladness that the plight of some Urban Indigenous people was finally being acknowledged as she read Rory's words.

"The Indian Act" was carefully worded to exclude most of the Indigenous people of Canada from forever being able to match the requirements for membership in Indian Bands. First the Metis, the people who had any trace of the French or English blood of the mixed races that worked the fur trade for centuries were not placed on Band lists when the infamous numbered treaties were negotiated. During the Treaty negotiations the Commissioners themselves decided who was Status Indian and who was Metis. The procedure was extremely problematic as the Commissioners decided arbitrarily on who was Metis by things like skin color alone. The ones labeled Metis were given scrip for land instead that government officials knew would likely be sold immediately to speculators accompanying or getting to treating making places ahead of the treaty negotiators.

That way the government of Canada would not have any treaty obligations to them in the future. In most cases, with hunting and trapping land now becoming ranch and settler land, they became a landless, wandering group of people on the fringes of settler towns obtaining whatever low paying jobs that became available in the settler population or trying to survive by hunting and trapping in extremely remote areas.

As well, female members of Indian Bands were seriously discriminated against. Male members could marry a white woman and retain status but females who married white men were excluded from membership as well as any children they produced or even had from previous Status mates. It was only in 1978, as a result of a United Nations protest that females who had married white men could again seek status. This resulted in over one hundred thousand requests for reinstatement that caused chaos on reserve communities with scare land and re-sources. Even if membership was allowed it would only be for one generation of children not forever.

Members of Indian Bands were forcefully removed if they became professional people. Ways were forever being found to eliminate people off Band lists. The result now is that large numbers of Indigenous people, (an estimated sixty percent) have only privately funded non-government organizations to rely on for need in the large Urban Centers of Canada. They still have to cope with the negative Indian stereotypes from a Canadian pop-ulation that still largely enjoys white privilege (being viewed favorably for rentals, post-secondary entrance, jobs, friendship and group memberships). They also tend to be blended in with other visible minorities by others and are constantly having to answer people's demands as to who they are, which because of Identity confusion is often very hard to do.

"Well do you think this shopping center has any hope of being successful?" Kate was startled by Bill Mason's question at the end of her narration.

"Why not?" Kate found herself answering. "It's within walking room of the large municipality of Delta and streams of people go by this location every day to and from the ferries to Vancouver Island. Besides huge retailers have already agreed to anchor the center and I'm sure high-status First Nations Designers, artists and musicians will be featured in the stores. Maybe even non-status Indigenous people can find employment as well as sons and daughters of Tsawwassen Band Members. That would be a first."

"I don't know. People are always rushing to and rushing off of ferries around this location. I'm not sure they will take the time to stop at the shopping Center."

"The Tourist Bureaus use Aboriginal Art as a draw for B.C. Tourism all over the world. Just look at Bill Reid's and other First Nations Artist's work at the Vancouver Airport. I'm sure tourists will come from all over the world just to stop at the Tsawwassen Center."

Several days later Kate realized that Bill Mason was looking really odd as he sat at one of the lap-top computers in one of the hotel rooms they were staying at.

"What's the problem, Bill?"

"Look at this e-mail? We are all summoned to a meeting tomorrow at McBay Resources Offices. I think someone has finally gotten around to looking at the latest series of filming I've sent them."

"Bring all Company equipment with you and return any rental vehicles or equipment to their owners. Cancel any film locations you have booked in advance and any extras you have hired."

"I think we are being terminated," Bill confessed as Rory came into the room.

"I was afraid of this," Kate and Rory looked at each other. "You two have been much too positive about the B.C. Treaties we have been filming. I knew Chuck McBay was expecting different results. I had better go and cancel everything."

"I guess we've done ourselves in," Rory chuckled. "But I've saved enough for the first year of a Ph.D. program. How about you?"

"I guess so," Kate acknowledged.

Chapter 7. Retribution.

Kate realized there was no welcome wagon this time as she sat down in Arthur McBay's reception area. She was relieved that they had been summoned to the McBay Resources offices instead of Rory's apartment.

"Mr. McBay will see you now," the receptionist frostily summoned Bill Mason, Rory and herself into the inner office. Kate sighed in relief as George McBay was not present. Arthur and his father were seated behind a large desk and glared at the trio as they entered.

"You are all fired! Kate's ears rang in protest as the senior McBay yelled at them. Arthur thrust envelopes at them. Kate opened hers and was delighted to find a large severance packet. In it was a letter requiring signatures that they had been paid in full and would not divulge anything that had been said or done while under the McBay's employment.

"They are putting us under a gag notice," Rory whispered.

"You'll notice that those documents are in your real names," Chuck McBay sneered. I've paid you a large sum of money in the severance policy to avoid slanderous accusations. We've had private detectives looking into your backgrounds. Kate shivered as the elder McBay pronounced her and Rory's real names. "Katherine Golden Eagle and Rory Broken Head, no wonder we got glowing reports of recent B. C. Treaties. Make sure you sign those promises to never reveal anything concerning the making of this documentary. I don't want George's name bandied about when I destroy the last part of the documentary."

"I think you should destroy the whole documentary," Arthur's voice demanded.

Kate prayed that he would, it was so unbalanced.

"Nonsense. The rest of the film says what I wanted said about our distant relative David Laird and my hero Duncan Campbell Scott. We'll shoot a few more scenes interviewing influential people that agree with our views on the continued welfare dependency of Indian people from these ill-conceived, modern treaties and submit the completed project to the Toronto Film Festival. George will be happy with what I have done when he gets back from his Honeymoon."

"George doesn't know about this?" Kate realized Arthur McBay's voice was incredulous.

"I'm saving it for a wedding present. When he realizes his narrator and his history expert were misleading him even about their names and then stabbed him in the back with the last scenes of the film he will be grateful I saved him from disaster yet again."

Kate felt like she had been punched in the stomach. Her fears were coming true. She and Rory were responsible for a totally unbalanced documentary about Confederation's effect on the Aboriginal people.

Later, over dinner Rory tried to lift her heavy mood.

"Don't worry, Kate, no one will know who Kiana Kealoha really is or where she has gone. Chuck McBay will never release our real names. You could even start to wear glasses again. Just put non-prescription lenses in them."

"Our film careers are over," Bill Mason complained, downing a second glass of whiskey. I wonder who Chuck McBay will hire to re-do those last scenes.

"Something will come along Bill," Kate realized that Rory was trying to cheer both of them up.

"Remember the old adage that when one door closes, another opens and speaking about doors I'm going to send off a request to go directly into a Ph.D. program without finishing my Masters. You should do the same, Kate, and we'll pick up where we left off with the Mosaic Awareness Scale and the World View Quilt Patterns. I think we have enough money for the start of the program anyway."

"You could lose everything that way," Bill Mason warned. "If you don't manage to finish your Doctorate you'll not have the Masters of Art either. Most graduate students in Canada take the other way and complete their Masters first. It's in the States that a lot of students jump into the Doctorate programs without finishing the Masters first."

Kate suddenly remembered Luke Spencer's words on the plane ride they had shared.

Sometimes you have to jump into the canoe alone, she remembered. *At least Rory wants to be in this canoe with me.*

"I'll send off a letter to the Dean tomorrow," she promised. "Maybe we can do some research on developing Core Emotional Resiliency Programs for Indigenous People as well." Kate suddenly realized that her back pain had miraculously disappeared.

"Core Emotional Resiliency training," I like that. Maybe my brother wouldn't have died if he had received training in that."

"You know Rory, you're right. That Sciatica Nerve pain that I have must be is Psychosomatic. It went away when I realized we would both be in the Doctorate Program together. We can support each other's point of view."

"Exactly."

Two months later as Kiana came into the rental suite near the University that she was now sharing with Rory the sound of her answering machine reached her ears.

I hope that's not another message from George McBay, Kate thought as she put the groceries down. *Imagine him leaving a message to call as if nothing had happened since that night he seduced me. Rory was right to tell me just to completely ignore the louse.* Kate pressed the Play button and was astonished to hear George McBay's voice again.

"Hi Beautiful. Would you give me a call? I need you to narrate some films Father insists I re-do. Of course I look forward to seeing you again as well. Looking forward to hearing from you.

George."

Oh My God, Kate thought. She quickly erased George's message. *Maybe I had better tell Rory what happened that night. We're just sharing quarters to save money but George McBay might call again and leave even more incriminating messages. Maybe I should phone George and tell him to never leave a message again.*

No, she decided. *This is another hostage taking incident. I'm not going to go through any more toxic conversations with George McBay. He's deranged. I'll just ignore him. Surely he will get the message this time. Surely he's not going to humiliate himself further by leaving another message.*

Kate was startled as Rory suddenly came in the door.

"Guess what," she managed. "Another message from George McBay. He wants to hire me to redo some scenes that his father wants him to re-shoot."

"My God! I trust you are Just going to ignore him again."

"You can believe that for sure."

"By the way Kate, I think we should redo the name of the Mosaic Awareness Scale to Awareness of Canadian Aboriginal History Scale. That will fit better with my Quilt Patterns of World Views In Canada Since Pre- Contact."

"That's a good idea."

"We can still use UFC Categories like Fly Weight or Bantom Weight but let's think about what questions we should put in the Awareness of Canadian Aboriginal History Scale." Kate sat down at the adjoining desk in the small living area.

"This is so much fun," she mused. *Working so closely with Rory on a joint dissertation topic. He's still too analytic but maybe I can get him to open up his heart at some point. I'll just try and be as unconditionally loving as possible.*

SUGGESTED FURTHER READING.

Daschuk, James; "Clearing The Plains: Disease, Politicis of Starvation, And The Loss of Aboriginal Life";
University of Regina Press, Regina, Saskatchewan, 2013.
Flexner, James Thomas; "Mohawk Baronet: A Biography of Sir William Johnson:" Syracuse University Press; 1979.
King, Thomas; "The Inconvenient Indian: A Curious Account Of Native People In North America;" Anchor Canada, 2013.
Miller, J. R.; "Compact, Contract, Covenant: Aboriginal Treaty-Making in Canada;" University of Toronto Press, Toronto, 2009.

Made in the USA
Charleston, SC
29 August 2014